Van Go

Van Gogh In Paris

✦

A Novel

Nicholas Vazzana

iUniverse, Inc.
New York Lincoln Shanghai

Van Gogh In Paris
A Novel

iUniverse books may be ordered through booksellers or by contacting:

iUniverse
2021 Pine Lake Road, Suite 100
Lincoln, NE 68512
www.iuniverse.com
1-800-Authors (1-800-288-4677)

Because of the dynamic nature of the Internet, any Web addresses or links contained in this book may have changed since publication and may no longer be valid.

This is a work of fiction. All of the characters, names, incidents, organizations, and dialogue in this novel are either the products of the author's imagination or are used fictitiously.

ISBN: 978-0-595-44160-0 (pbk)
ISBN: 978-0-595-88485-8 (ebk)

Printed in the United States of America

For my wife, Elaine, my best friend,

and for my mother, Marguerite, who will always be there.

If you are lucky enough to have lived in Paris as a young man,
then wherever you go for the rest of your life, it stays with you,
for Paris is a moveable feast.

—Ernest Hemingway

Historical Note

Most of the historical information that exists about Vincent van Gogh is based on the correspondence with his brother Theo. When the artist came to Paris and moved in with Theo unexpectedly in early 1886, the letters ended. Therefore, much of Vincent's two years in Montmartre, the pleasure center of Paris, cannot be documented. Most biographers and novelists have devoted very little attention to this period in the artist's life.

However, the twenty-four-month stay in Montmartre had a profound effect on this thirty-three-year-old Dutchman. He blossomed as a painter, developed his own style, and interrelated with many of the great artists of *La Belle Epoque*. He also matured as a social being, experiencing the complex emotions of friendship, affection, and sex, some for the first time. Unfortunately, his physical and mental health began to deteriorate during this period—and his dependency on absinthe, the powerful liqueur known as "the green fairy," would change his life.

Later, medical science would determine that absinthe was a highly toxic, analgesic narcotic. The drink was found to be so harmful that it was banned by every Western nation, including France and the United States, by 1914. This move was very controversial among many writers and artists, who claimed they received their inspiration and creativity from "the green fairy."

We will never know to what extent van Gogh's physical and mental health was affected by his drinking. Some authorities speculate that the artist may have developed alcoholic epilepsy. At various points in his life, he also exhibited the classic signs of schizophrenia, bipolar disorder, or acute attention-deficit disorder. Any of these conditions could have caused van Gogh's inability to function within society, the hypersensitivity of his senses, and the highs and lows of manic depression. No one can be certain of Vincent's disorder because diagnosis and treatment for these conditions were not available in the 1880s.

Through extensive research, including information provided on the Internet by art museums around the world, I have attempted to piece together a fictionalized but plausible account of van Gogh's time in Paris. I was drawn to the subject because I am an artist myself. As with many biographical novels, the dialogue of the story has been created, but most of the events follow the general historical timeline of the artist's travels. After reading much about van Gogh's life, this is how I imagined he lived his life in Montmartre.

Van Gogh was a complex individual, never conforming to any stereotype. He arrived unexpectedly in Paris and left just as abruptly. But he lived those two years like a ball of kinetic energy, interacting with the nineteenth century's most dynamic artistic and intellectual environment.

Prologue

◆

1890—Outside the Village
of Auvers-sur-Oise, Near Paris

He was stretched out among the tall stalks of a flowing wheat field. The screech of a circling crow was the only sound that pierced the warm July stillness. Through half-closed lashes, the Dutchman squinted at the blinding sun. Often in his painting, the artist would look asquint at scenes to capture the broad impressions of shape and color.

This day, through blurred vision appeared flashes of the painter's favorite colors—warm yellow, vermilion, and violet. The vivid hues dissolved into familiar hallucinations: an exotic woman dancing with a tambourine, a child crying in a cradle, and angry faces of men yelling. Then, like a chemical reaction, all were replaced by his paintings and their profusion of blue skies, brilliant flowers, and ultramarine waters.

Out loud, he cursed his art. "You miserable beast, the work that is never finished. I paint a new *dieu damne* canvas every day, but now I am done. I've tried every technique, every color. There are no more surprises. The work is finished, and the beast is all I have."

While attempting to rise and walk a few steps to his easel, the artist fell and instinctively grabbed for the canvas. The easel, palette, and its bright paints splattered to the ground. A small bottle of absinthe tumbled from the artist's pocket, shattering against a metal object before coming to rest in the grass. The sticky, emerald liqueur coated the handle of the steel-gray pistol. And the green fairy seeped into the soil, where the despairing artist could not pursue or be enchanted by her promises.

1

Four Years Earlier

Le Express from Antwerp to Paris was on time as it dashed through the French countryside in an early March snow. Sitting by the window, Vincent Willem van Gogh watched the trees emerge as twisted black forms highlighted by the white flurries. His light green eyes jumped along the wet, lifeless branches as they flew past.

The passenger looked haggard and restless. His ruddy face was drawn and gaunt, accentuated by receding reddish-brown hair and a stubby beard. The thirty-three-year-old's facial expression was remote and inaccessible. This together with intelligent, deeply thoughtful eyes gave one the impression that he was pondering a profound philosophical question.

Between his knees sat a large cardboard box secured with twine, and he wore a farmer's jacket of sheepskin. But otherwise, he was just another immigrant in this *compartment* on the train. Many passengers were from northern Europe or Scandinavia, traveling south to make a better life. After all, this was *La Belle Epoque*, when Paris was becoming the center of Europe. It was a period of emerging prosperity, enterprise, and social freedom created by the effects of automation and mass production. There was more bread, wine, and clothing, together with new, fashionable department shores. The City of Lights was illuminating the world, and this was the place to be, no matter what occupation a person was pursuing.

A little Belgian boy and his mother sat across the compartment from van Gogh. The boy looked repeatedly into the man's lightly colored eyes. Although he was just a small boy, his stare made the immigrant uneasy. Eventually, Vincent smiled at the child, and the boy responded with an amiable grin that highlighted two missing baby teeth. Van Gogh's entire face brightened, taking on a look of contentment. He contemplated his fondest dream of someday marrying and perhaps having a child.

The boy's mother was a plump, bulky woman, no more than twenty, nursing an infant at her breast. In a firm voice, she commanded, "Piet, look out the window. Stop looking at the *laboureur* across the way!" She spoke in Flemish, but van Gogh understood. He knew many European languages and, despite his looks, was not a farm laborer.

The locomotive seemed to gain speed as it approached Ile de France, the large area surrounding Paris. On both sides of the train, van Gogh could see miles of wheat fields mixed with shallow mounds of snow. He suddenly imagined that the train had turned into a bird as it flew with the blowing snow over the dormant, broken fields. Train or bird, it was speeding him toward a new life.

"Snow—this far south? Only Copenhagen still gets snow in March." The words were German, but they were directed at van Gogh by an elderly Dane sitting to his right. He had a gentle face, a gray beard, and large, rough hands.

"No, it's still winter, and even Paris can get the cold from the north," responded van Gogh in German.

"I'm Borge, a craftsman from Denmark. I'm on my way to work at the porcelain factory in Rouen."

"I am Vincent, a painter, formerly of the Netherlands." He spoke in the rapid-fire cadence of someone with more on his mind than he could hope to verbalize. His words passed through his teeth with a slight whistling sound.

Small talk was difficult for the Dutchman, and the two fell silent listening to the clatter of the train's progress. Vincent turned away to look out the window, but the old man's manner and image, which reminded him of his father, an ordained minister who had recently died of a stroke, stayed in his thoughts. His mind flashed to an explosive confrontation with his father two years earlier.

"You're unfit to be a husband," declared Reverend Theodorus van Gogh. His steely gray eyes seemed to pierce his son's soul. "You'll be the damnation of Margot Begemann, a good woman."

The elder van Gogh was referring to an episode that had taken place following Vincent's announcement that he wanted to marry Margot, a pleasant but shy woman more than ten years his senior. Margot was one of four unmarried sisters who were neighbors to the van Gogh's in Nuenen, in the south of Holland. The couple often took long walks together and spoke about many subjects, including starting a family. Margot was very devoted to the fledgling artist and enjoyed watching him sketch the gentle landscapes in the vicinity.

Both families forbade the marriage because they thought Vincent should have an occupation other than painting, and he had a reputation for philandering with prostitutes. After their parents refused to give their blessing, Margot was so upset that she attempted suicide by swallowing strychnine during one of her walks with Vincent. When she collapsed, van Gogh got her to admit what she had taken. He then tried to get her to vomit before picking her up and carrying her to a doctor. Both families blamed Vincent for the incident even though he had obtained the medical treatment that had saved her life.

"You want to marry this troubled woman?" stormed the Reverend. "You do not have the moral understanding to support a family. You care only for your harlots. And you cannot even earn a living with your foolish paintings."

Those words had gone too far. Vincent's hard fist hit the stern, gray-haired minister squarely in the face. The punch knocked his father to the ground, and blood trickled from his nose and onto his white collar and gray cassock.

"Gare du Nord—the City of Paris! We'll be arriving in ten minutes!"

The conductor's words shook Vincent from his thoughts, drawing him back to the present. The journey was ending, but like any immigration, the end marked a new beginning, a chance to start over. Vincent viewed this fresh start as his last chance. As the train approached the terminal, his entire *histoire* emerged before him. Everything he had attempted to accomplish since childhood had somehow turned out badly. Recently, a local Catholic priest had accused van Gogh of impregnating a young woman. The charge was found to be untrue, but Vincent became more of an outcast and spoke with no one. Living at home was no longer possible, for his actions seemed to bring shame upon the family and made his own life miserable. Vincent was determined to either change his life or accept death as an alternative. As he sat on the train, this morbid thought reminded him of the words of the early English writer Thomas Browne:

Wee cannot fear death and also be afraide of life.
Thy trueste valour is to contemne death when life is more terrible than death.

Above all, Vincent van Gogh knew he had the desire, perseverance, and fortitude to become a great artist. It was a highly competitive field in which very few succeeded. But no matter what it required, the Dutchman was willing to pay the price. This journey was only the start of a campaign to acquire a mastery of skills from the greatest painters of the age. He was determined to be accepted at a leading school of fine arts in Paris. Furthermore, he knew that he would never return to the Netherlands.

As the train slowed, Vincent was relieved that the snow was ending. Nonetheless, considering the baggage he had to carry, the walk through Paris to Theo's office would be arduous. He was looking forward to seeing his younger brother, who had always sheltered him from the difficulties brought about by Vincent's abiding antisocial behavior.

The train came to an abrupt stop at Gare du Nord Terminal. Passengers jumped to their feet and started to exit the railroad car. Like many of his fellow immigrants, van Gogh was traveling with most of his worldly possessions. In addition to the box between his knees, Vincent grabbed a large sack and a leather cap stored in the luggage holder above his seat. The faded and weather-scarred hat was actually a miner's cap given to him during his travels in Belgium seven years earlier. Wearing the hat, he followed the noisy crowd out of the train and into the station.

The melted snow had bestowed a dirty sheen on the gritty Boulevard de Denain outside Gare du Nord. The somber, gray afternoon seemed to correspond to the gray-black buildings standing off the boulevard. Everywhere, adults, children, suitcases, and horse-drawn carriages moved in different directions. Van Gogh had been to Paris more than ten years before, but it looked like a different city, especially in all the confusion.

The Dutchman asked a burly porter in French where he might find Boulevard Montmarte. The man only pointed to the south and mumbled, "Bonne Nouvelle," referring to an upscale neighborhood among the grand boulevards of Paris. The artist vaguely remembered the area and proceeded in the direction of the porter's finger.

Crossing the busy boulevard was difficult, with the armada of horse-drawn cabriolets, or cabs, filling the roadway. The deafening staccato sounds of hooves on the cobblestones shook the street beneath the artist's feet as he darted across with his belongings. The sound of a cracking whip propelled him onto the smooth pavers of the sidewalk as the black coach box of a cab rumbled past.

Despite the traffic and confusion, van Gogh could sense that he was walking toward the center of a well-planned city. Similar to a finely composed painting, everything performed according to a predestined function. A sea of mansard roofs stretched out before him like the ocean. Streets emulated pulsating arteries under a vibrant skin as turnabouts controlled traffic like the hub of a wheel. Through his raw senses, the traveler could feel the life-giving energy and heartbeat of Paris. Even though the air was chilly, Vincent could smell the diverse warm aromas emanating from this prodigious city.

The streets and squares were accented by *enchanteur* ladies strolling alongside their Parisian gentlemen in dark frock coats and silk top hats. A fresh mist had just begun, and Vincent started to slip on the greasy pavement as a few black umbrellas started to spring open. After a while, sharing the narrow sidewalk with all the umbrellas became difficult.

Finally, he reached Boulevard Montmarte, but the weight of the cardboard box had become unbearable, so he rested his belongings on the sidewalk. Compared to the area leading southward from Gare du Nord, this neighborhood was more upscale and its pedestrians more affluent. The rain stopped, and the air over the grand boulevard shimmered with vibrant colors.

Actually, the elegance and sophistication of the atmosphere could be traced back to *Cité Prefect* Baron Haussmann, who was commissioned by Napoleon III to modernize Paris. He replaced the old twisting streets and rundown apartment houses with wide, tree-lined boulevards and expansive gardens. Haussmann's reconstruction of Paris had changed more than 60 percent of the historic city.

Boulevard Montmartre had been completely renovated into a wide thoroughfare with broad sidewalks and advertising kiosks on every corner. A line of gaslights perched on tall poles separated two tracks for omnibuses, cabs, and lorries. Trees shielded the sidewalks from the roadway.

Feeling somewhat out of place, the artist picked up the box and sack and continued walking alongside the other pedestrians down the boulevard. He felt lonely in the crowd, like a rural Northerner who did not fit into the Parisian lifestyle. The shops along the sidewalk were quite attractive with bright displays in their clear plate-glass windows. The glittering gold of a jewelry shop, a milliner's light-colored silks, and a florist's rainbow of blossoms stimulated the artist's sensibilities. Vincent was captivated by the strong scent of Italian leather at the clothier, the rising aroma of vanilla from the confectioner's shop, and the essence of jasmine emanating from the perfume boutique.

The next store front offered no sights or scents to gain his attention, and he almost walked past number nineteen. But he looked up in time at the awning to see "Boussod & Valadon (Formerly Goupil & CIE)" in gold letters. From the sidewalk, Vincent could see several large paintings inside the shop. The sunny front window was no place for valuable paintings.

Upon entering through a glass door, he triggered a little bell that announced his intrusion. A young sales associate approached. "*Bonjour*! Do you have a delivery for the gallery?"

"I have no delivery," responded the traveler in a hostile tone. "My brother, Theo, is *directeur* here. Tell him I have arrived."

"Oh, Monsieur van Gogh, I am Leon, but I regret that your brother is not in the gallery. He attends the midday *déjeuner* with business clients, and I do not know when he will return."

"Then, I shall leave him a note. Leon, tell Monsieur van Gogh I shall be at the Louvre. Give me some writing paper, and place my possessions in his office for the afternoon."

"Ah, *oui*, monsieur."

2

Dressed as a gentleman in his frock coat with stiff, winged collar and beige cravat, Theodore van Gogh entered Cour Napoleon of the Musée du Louvre. Unlike his brother, Theo appeared a mild-mannered, dignified man of conservative Protestant habits. Not outwardly adventurous, Vincent's younger brother found it difficult to defy any element of convention or propriety.

Just as the note specified, Vincent met his brother in the museum's Dutch and Flemish salon of sixteenth and seventeenth-century art. Vincent was sitting on a broad bench and gazing at a self-portrait by Rembrandt that dated from the sad, later years of the old master's bankruptcy. The demeanor on Vincent's face seemed to conform to Rembrandt's depressed, thoughtful countenance.

"Cent, my dear brother, when did you arrive in Paris?" Theo asked. "Did … did you come for a visit?"

The weary Vincent rose from the bench and stared at him while trying to make sense of his brother's question. He thought Theo would realize that he had come to Paris to live.

"No," Vincent replied. "I have come to stay with you, as I have written in my letters."

"My brother, I thought you were only referring to the possibility later in the year. Currently, I reside in just a single room, hardly enough space for one person."

Vincent panicked and his eyes suddenly moistened with tears. Even though it was cool in the museum, perspiration appeared on his brow, and his breathing became shallow.

As he had always done, Theo blamed himself for the reaction. Like a parent who is sorry for using harsh words with a child, he felt only remorse for his choice of words.

"Please, come sit down," Theo pleaded as he took Vincent's arm and encouraged his brother to sit beside him on the bench.

Visibly agitated, Vincent broke from Theo's touch and yelled loudly, "You little bastard, you're telling me I should not have come! Well, I don't need you. I'll find my own way!"

"Vincent, please, you're going to get us ejected from the museum," said Theo as he tried to change the subject. "Let's go. We'll get your things at my office, and we'll go to my flat."

Vincent was relieved by Theo's suggestion but only responded, "Perhaps I shall stay with you for a brief time until I get back on my feet and sell some of my paintings."

"Of course, Cent, you can stay with me as long as necessary. Let us heat some coffee and eat a fresh baguette with ham."

After retrieving Vincent's belongings from the gallery, the brothers walked to Rue Fontaine and waited for an omnibus for the trip north, away from the grand boulevards of central Paris. After a few minutes, the large public coach rattled its way into view. Drawn by two large workhorses, the massive tram was filled with nearly thirty passengers riding home after a typical workday. Some rode on benches perched on the roof.

Theo led his brother onto the omnibus through the rear entrance. Inside, a wide variety of city dwellers sat knee-to-knee on wooden benches that ran down the sides of the vehicle. The brothers found a space for themselves and the baggage that they carried.

Vincent was surprised by the tight quarters in which passengers were squeezed together for the ride home. However, he was glad to sit and watch the scenery go by after walking all day. Rue Fontaine was a busy street with many cafes and stores, but it also had many little parks, squares, and quaint churches along the route.

The brothers headed toward Boulevard de Clichy in Montmartre. This was a working-class district on the city's outskirts known for its daring, often racy, entertainment industry that lured thrill-seeking Parisians to its dance halls and cabarets, circuses, and brothels.

Theo chose to live in Montmartre because of its raucous spirit and free lifestyle. He enjoyed an exciting life that seemed to contradict his conservative disposition. Theo appreciated the unusual mix of people drawn to the quarter, including avant-garde artists and students, performers seeking fame and fortune, and working-class laborers attracted by inexpensive housing.

Montmartre, also known as La Buttes, was situated around a hill about a hundred thirty meters high with little streets winding up to the top. The streets below the hill were busy with people rushing around during the day. On top of the butte, life was simpler and bucolic with windmills, large gardens, and grazing sheep and cows.

In Roman history, the hill was called *Mons Mercurii*, the mountain of Mercury, the god of trade. Most believe that the name "Montmartre" comes from *mons martyrium*, meaning "hill of the martyrs." In AD 272, three saints—Denis, Rustique, and Eleuthere—were sentenced to death by the Roman emperor Auretianus. Saint Denis, the first bishop of Paris, Saint Rustique, archpriest, and Saint Eleuthere, archdeacon, were first tortured on the Ile de la Cité. They were then brought to the foot of Mons Mercurii, later named Rue des Abbesses, where they were beheaded. Legend has it that Saint Denis picked up his head, washed away the blood, and walked uphill to the place where the cathedral of Saint Denis would later be built.

3

After the brothers arrived at the small flat in Montmarte, Vincent sat silently in a chair, rubbing his hands quickly together in a circular motion. This reaction was not a result just of the cold but was often exhibited by the sensitive artist during periods of stress or confrontation. Theo tried not to look at his brother as he lit the large iron stove in his *appartement* on Rue de Laval. The flat, which was really just one large room, was still quite cold, because Theo had not been there all day. Once the fire started, the room quickly filled with a friendlier, more reassuring warmth. Vincent stood up and took off his sheepskin jacket, hanging it on a hook behind the door.

"Paris has changed since I was here last in the seventies."

"I know you despised it from your letters," said Theo. "Weren't you in your religious phase at the time?"

"Yes, indeed. I spent my time translating the Bible into English, what a waste of time that was."

"Well, the city, as well as yourself, has changed since that time. It's now the greatest city in the world. And this area, Montmarte, is the center of the artistic life of Europe, the model of a free, bohemian existence."

While listening to Theo's words, Vincent stepped over to the window. As he contemplated the sprinkling of lights that were coming on all over the neighborhood, he took out his pipe and lit it. He was beginning to feel good about the atmosphere of the neighborhood. "How are things going at the gallery, little brother?"

"Excellent. I just sold another Millet."

Theo van Gogh was progressing relatively well in his position at the gallery, which was formerly owned by Goupil & Company. Messieurs Boussod and Valadon, the new owners, were very pleased with Theo's thorough knowledge of art and his keen ability to sell contemporary paintings. Consequently, for more than six years, Theo had been sending his older brother a hundred and fifty francs a month, which paid for all of Vincent's living expenses. Even before, Theo had always been there for his older brother as the buffer between the harsh reality of life and his apparent inability to function within his surroundings.

When the coffee was ready, Theo prepared a little meal with bread and meat and some soup. The two men sat at a little square table in the corner of the room, eating their food.

"This is very good bread. It smells freshly baked," said the artist, devouring the long thin sandwich made with strips of ham covered with salted butter. "This is the first food I've had since the beer and hard rolls of last night."

While they ate, Theo brought out a carafe of neighborhood wine. The little dinner was capped off by some fruit and cheese that Theo had been saving for a special treat. Vincent ate like a starving child.

With food in his stomach and wine inspiring his head, Vincent spoke from his heart. "Theo, I realize that I haven't been a very good brother to you. But things are going to be different. On the train ride from Antwerp, I had this feeling that my entire life would change. I was leaving my old life behind and devoting myself exclusively to learning how to express the art inside of me."

Theo was also in a talkative mood. "Cent, you have come to the right place. Montmartre is like a dream come true. If Paris is the City of Lights, Montmartre is its enlightenment. Painters, writers, and entertainers are creating things here that the world has never known. This is it, the center of our civilization."

Vincent listened in rapt attention, pouring himself more wine and puffing on his pipe. He wanted to hear more.

"You just walk down the street and see painters like Renoir, Pissarro, and Degas and the student artists of the ateliers—the teaching art schools. And when you live in the area, you discover that everyone is friendly and sociable, nothing like the grand boulevards of central Paris."

Remembering Theo's letters, Vincent asked, "Where is that school of fine art in Montmartre? I believe it's called Atelier Cormon. You said Professeur Cormon's reputation and quality of instruction are among the best in Paris."

"Yes, it's on the local boulevard. I've already spoken to the professeur about you and brought some of your work. It's probably one of the best places to enroll, if you want to learn from a master academic painter."

"Theo, it's not just the wine. I feel a thorough sense of exhilaration. It is as if destiny has brought me to this place and time."

"My brother, I feel it also. You are in the right place," said Theo, pointing out the window. "If you went on top of this building and threw paint, you could reach half of the future great artists of the world."

For the rest of the evening, the two men sat at the small table in the corner of the room, drinking wine and speaking about art, particularly that of the Impressionist painters. Vincent had not yet seen any original work, but Theo insisted that Impressionism was an important development in moderne art.

Vincent avoided any talk of family or of the people back home. He no longer felt like a Northerner. The south would be his home permanently. Theo wanted to believe that the move would resolve Vincent's insecurities and mental turmoil, but he knew that was more than anyone could expect.

4

Vincent awoke to the cold, gray morning. Sitting up in bed, he wrapped a blanket around his thick, firm body, which resembled that of an ironworker rather than that of an artist. Dancing along the cold floor, he quickly crossed the room and lit both the heat stove and his pipe. The sound of Theo's congested breathing and occasional coughing broke the silence. Not attempting to awaken him, Vincent began to unpack his baggage.

Vincent found his large box and cut the twine to open it. Inside was a jumbled mess of art supplies, books, shoes, clothing, and disassembled wooden frames. There were also about fifty rolled-up canvases of various sizes, and arranged under rigid mats were several Japanese wood prints and hundreds of his pencil drawings.

"Belongings, like people, can only burden a man and restrict his progress," he thought while looking at the pile of his meager possessions. But then he began to think about the *Borinage* in Belgium, where the peasants he had met possessed nothing but the torn, dirty clothes on their backs.

"I still cannot feel the cool water in my mouth!"

"Don't upset yourself. You're drinking the water, but you must swallow, or you'll choke," said van Gogh, as he held a cup of water to the miner's burned lips. It was eight years before, and Vincent was serving as an evangelist in the mining district of southern Belgium near the French border known as the *Borinage*. This impoverished area was unlike any other in Europe. Most of the wretched inhabitants either died in horrendous coal-mining accidents or from starvation, epidemics, or the cold.

Working as a lay preacher, the Dutchman was the only person to volunteer to care for the man, who had been critically burned from a firedamp explosion in a coal mine. He nursed the miner every day for three months before he died.

Vincent was eager to share the suffering of the miners and their families after reading Dostoyevsky's *The Idiot*, the story of innocent Prince Myshkin, a good man who learned to achieve humiliation and suffering before he could be considered the ideal man. The prince was a spiritual character, while those around him were more concerned with wealth and sensual pleasures.

Watching over the miner, van Gogh remembered the passage from *The Idiot* when a dying man asked Myshkin, "How can I achieve an honorable death?"

The prince replied, "You can pass by us and forgive us our happiness."

Vincent was so possessed by the personal quest to develop his spiritual nature that he gave away most of his money, clothing, and belongings to the unfortunate peasants. He wore ragged clothes and lived like a hermit. The miners, who were mostly French-speaking Catholics, called Vincent "the Dutch-Protestant Saint Francis." Suspicious, local authorities were not as complimentary and after a brief investigation declared him a religious fanatic.

The church officials who had sent him to the Borinage also became alarmed and issued a report that applauded his saintly qualities of charity, kindness, and faith but said he did not demonstrate the appropriate attributes of a minister. The officials cited his unorthodox behavior and improper image, as well as his apparent inability to deliver a sermon before his congregation. He was withdrawn and self-conscious in front of large groups, often forgetting what he wanted to say. However, he was able to relate with the miners on an individual basis. Even though Vincent was dismissed, he stayed in the Borinage for another six months, working with the poor without pay or support from any higher authority.

"It is pleasant to awaken in a warm room." Theo yawned as he opened his eyes and stretched his arms and legs. "What is the state of the *météorologique* today?"

Looking from the window, Vincent reported, "Just like yesterday … miserable, damp, and possibly snow. What do you expect? It is only the beginning of March." Without pausing for a breath, Vincent added, "I hope we can get to see Monsieur Cormon today."

Theo remembered the conversation of the night before about the teaching studio, but he did not care to think about it first thing in the morning. "Fernand Cormon will not see you without current samples of your work."

"I have them right here, dragged all the way from Antwerp." Vincent started fumbling through the materials in the box. He selected five drawings and one canvas, a work completed about ten months ago, of which he was most proud. He unraveled the canvas and handed it to Theo. It was a very dark painting depicting five squalid, destitute peasants unhappily sitting at a dimly lit table and eating potatoes. "Do you think I have captured the honesty of these farmers?"

Theo did not answer quickly. As a professional art dealer, he recognized that the rural subject matter might appeal to his urban clientele, but he thought the painting brought out the hopelessness of life. He felt it was depressing, and its peasants looked grotesque.

"Vincent, what do you mean by honesty?"

The artist got a stern look on his face and raised his voice. "The honesty is obvious, you fool! These people, eating their potatoes in the lamplight, have dug the earth with those very hands they put in the dish. They have honestly earned their food."

At that moment, Theo was fearful that the old Vincent from the north had returned. He knew that his brother could change a peaceful morning into a turbulent day if steps were not taken to modify his behavior.

"Vincent, before we go to Boulevard de Clichy to see Monsieur Cormon, we have to establish some rules of conduct, if you are going to be admitted to this atelier. The other students are from an entirely different background than you. Many have had formal academic training. They dress well and are respectful of the relationship of student to instructor. If only to gain acceptance, you have to put forth a favorable image."

"I don't concur. You know me, Theo. I cannot appear to be someone I am not."

"And your clothing is deplorable. *Les misérables* of the maquis, the shacks on top of the hill, dress better than you."

"People either accept me for who I am, or they do not accept me. I care not what the bourgeoisie think."

"Vincent, with that attitude, you are defeating the very purpose of coming to Paris. You have said it yourself; you want to learn how the great painters express their art and to master the techniques and the realization. How can you succeed if you wall yourself away from the world of great art and great artists? I've never said it before, but Vincent, you know this is your last chance. You are thirty-three years old, and you have lived most of your life like a hermit. It's time you entered the real world. Do you hear what I'm saying, you poor miserable asshole?"

Theo's outspokenness jolted Vincent. He thought his younger brother had gone too far. Theo had now joined the enemy, the army of relatives who thought Vincent was mentally unstable and would never amount to anything. Vincent walked toward Theo and ripped the painting out of his hands. Theo jumped back as if his brother was about to strike him.

"I should have never come here. You're just like all the others. Now you want me to jump to your tune and live my life on your terms."

After regaining his composure, Theo spoke. "Vincent, I am not going to bring you to Cormon. You go by yourself. I refuse to embarrass myself and my employer in front of the dignified artists at that atelier. Either you try to be courteous and presentable today, or you go by yourself to Cormon."

Theo's threat seemed to instantly challenge Vincent's insecurities. "Theo, you know I cannot go alone to Cormon. I'm not very good with superiors in an interview situation. Okay, I'll be courteous, but you must accompany me."

"Then it's agreed, my brother, but we also have to make you look presentable. The first thing you should do is shave your beard. It shall make you look younger."

"And I'll resemble the bourgeois schoolboys whom I shall be spending my days with."

"No, Cent, you are in Paris, not the Borinage. Artists are considered cultured and progressive here, and most dress as gentlemen. They are respected, and they respect others. In Paris, a painter's image can get him farther than a paintbrush."

"But I do not have any gentleman's finery."

"Do not worry, Cent. I have a new suit of clothes, recently purchased, that you can wear for the interview."

Vincent took a deep breath. He was embarking on a new direction in his life. Inwardly, he was relieved that Theo had thrown him a lifeline that he was able to accept.

5

As the brothers strode down the wide sidewalk of Boulevard de Clichy on their way to Cormon's atelier, they braced themselves against a cold breeze. Vincent had just finished mounting the canvas of the painting, which he called *The Potato Eaters*, onto a wooden stretcher frame. Little nails fastened the canvas to the frame. It was difficult for Vincent to hold the large painting in the wind. Under his arm, Theo carried a portfolio of Vincent's drawings.

As he looked for number 104, Theo reminded his brother that he would do most of the talking to Monsieur Cormon. "I know the man very well from the time he painted the masterwork *The Family of Cane Escaping* and exhibited at the Salon. Remember, you've asked me to act as your agent in selling your paintings, and that includes making the initial contacts."

It was a tactful approach that did not offend the high-strung artist but would be crucial in acquiring acceptance to this prestigious teaching studio. Actually, the idea reflected a fundamental axiom of the art world—the presence of the painter often prevents the sale of the painting.

At 104, they came to a four-story building which was a converted factory. On the top floor was Cormon's atelier, where about thirty students were working in two large rooms. Most were working alone, while some were grouped together. Some were concerned with charcoal or pencil drawings, while others were pursuing oil painting at their easels. Most worked while viewing a model on a posing platform. Today, there were two models, one in each salon. A female sat naked on a backless chair, and a muscular man struck the pose of a Greek athlete throwing a discus.

Ceiling gaslights with reflectors were suspended every ten feet, but light flooded the atelier through the wall of glass windows and long skylights that ran the length of both studios. The walls, floors, and easels were splattered with droplets of paint that bathed the rooms in a gray-brown wash. Through the windows, they could see the rhythmical movement of young ballerinas practicing in their studios on the same floor in the building across the alleyway. It was a charming distraction that added a graceful refinement to the atelier's atmosphere.

The two visitors removed their coats as a receptionist showed them into a small office used by the directeur for individual conferences. Wearing borrowed clothing from his fraternal agent, Vincent looked quite handsome in a dark jacket, waistcoat, and white collar with dark green cravat. His face was smoothly shaven and his reddish brown hair was neatly brushed. The two were obviously brothers, except Theo did look a bit younger with his closely cropped half-beard and neatly parted brown hair.

"Good morning, gentlemen," Fernand Cormon said as he entered the room. He was a tall, thin gentleman about forty with dark rings about his friendly brown eyes. With thin black hair parted in the middle, he sported a groomed moustache and goatee. Looking at Vincent, he said, "Your brother has shown me your work from time to time, Monsieur van Gogh …"

Before Cormon could complete his thought, the older brother interrupted. "I am not van Gogh. My name is Vincent. Monsieur van Gogh was my father, and he is dead."

The silence was deafening, and a sinking feeling overcame Theo. The interview was starting off badly. Quickly, he blurted out, "Ah yes, we do not deal in formalities in our family. Vincent is a very friendly sort."

Thankfully, Cormon viewed Vincent's comment as an awkward attempt at humor. He noticed that his visitors had brought a painting and some drawings. "Are these samples of your latest work?"

Vincent answered, "Oui, Professeur Cormon. The painting was done ten months ago in Nuenen, Holland, before I went to Antwerp."

Theo added, "Monsieur le directeur, as you can see, he's done quite well with a difficult theme, the simple life of poor farmers."

Cormon did not react to Theo's critique and started to examine the drawings of Dutch cloth weavers, old men, and a country churchyard. As if in distant thought, he continued to view the materials before him and said finally, "Where and with whom have you studied?"

"I've had academic training from Master Anton Mauve of the School of the Hague and *Mijnheer* Anton Van Rappard, a Dutch instructor in Brussels. I have recently arrived from Antwerp, where I attended the Academy of Fine Arts for two months."

"Yes, I can discern the gray northern palette of Mauve and the Hague school in your work."

To avoid any unpleasant retort from Vincent, Theo interjected, "Anton Mauve is our cousin by marriage. He is a wonderful artist who has worked extensively with Vincent. Anton is having a very successful year with the Goupil Gallery in the Hague."

Turning his head from the samples, Cormon announced, "All right, Vincent, we will start you off in the intermediate class. The cost of instruction is twenty-five francs per month. Before you leave, you will take a list of materials and paints that you will bring to your first class the day after tomorrow."

Vincent smiled confidentially at Theo as he sat silently in his elegant attire and tight collar. Theo did not want to press their luck. "Professeur, thank you for your time. I'm sure my brother will acquire the fundamentals of classical art as a consequence of your highly regarded instruction."

Not wanting to be rushed out the door, Vincent added, "Monsieur Cormon, I know I'm considerably older than the other students here, but I'm extremely motivated to succeed and learn everything possible. May I observe your studio and examine the light?"

"Why, of course. You are a student here now, but please do not interrupt the students in their work. And, Monsieur van Gogh, I believe you'll go far in the world of art if you acquire the basics in academic instruction. You have a natural ability."

With that, Theo thanked the directeur again and ushered Vincent out of the cramped little room into one of the large salons where the students were working. As they entered the room, it appeared as if the female model and the artists were taking a late-morning break.

A striking, diminutive young man was holding hands with the laughing female model. The woman was standing in a dark red robe during the rest period in the drafty studio. She seemed to enjoy talking with the little man, who apparently was totally at ease in the company of attractive women.

Theo held his hand near his mouth and spoke quietly. "That, my brother, is Count Henri, the leader among the students and the unofficial mayor of Montmartre. He knows everyone and has relatives everywhere. You must meet him. The little count is also trying to make love to every woman in Paris."

The colorful Monsieur Henri was born Henri de Toulouse-Lautrec Monfa to a family of rank and privilege in Albi, an old city in southwest France. Count Alphonse and Countess Adele, his parents, could trace their lineage a thousand years back to the Age of Charlemagne. Actually, Alphonse and Adele were first cousins, as it was common for the aristocracy to intermarry within the same extended family. The countess was totally devoted to her son, and Alphonse was a flamboyant father who encouraged Henri in outdoor activities such as riding and hunting.

When Henri was only six, his father taught him the fundamentals of falcon hunting to encourage a love for the outdoors. Nonetheless, the boy was a frail child who was drawn to intellectual pursuits. Like other heirs of old nobility, Henri attended the finest schools and excelled in French literature, Latin, Greek, and English.

When Henry was fourteen, he had a slight fall in the woods at the family's Chateau du Bosc, north of Albi, and broke a leg at the thigh. About a year later, the same thing happened to the young nobleman's other leg. In both cases, the breaks did not heal properly, and Henri was not growing any taller. The family brought in top physicians who diagnosed the condition as a rare bone disease leading to short stature and permanent walking impairment. The diagnosis was correct. For as the young man approached adulthood, the upper body developed and grew slightly, while the legs atrophied. At twenty-one, Henri Toulouse-Lautrec would stand a little less than five feet tall and walk supported by a knotted cane.

Despite the handicap, Lautrec made the best of the abnormality. Witty and optimistic, the young man enjoyed reading, music, and, above all, drawing. He displayed a most even-tempered disposition despite occasional bouts of melancholy during long months of orthopedic treatment.

Rather than make him self-indulgent, the condition fostered a deep tolerance of the needs and feelings of other people. This brought the little count the love and respect of family, friends, and even servants. The result was that Monsieur Henri carried a self-confidence that would propel him through life, under his withered legs.

As Theo approached the modeling platform, he caught the eye of Lautrec.

"Bonjour, Monsieur Henri! You are looking well."

"If you consider this looking well, Monsieur van Gogh," quipped Henri, holding onto the female model's outstretched hand. Despite his size, his penetrating voice was deep and confident.

Lautrec held onto the woman with his left hand, as his right was supported by a short, cherry-wood cane. Henri appeared much younger than his twenty-one years. He wore a pince-nez and had dark hair and a dark complexion. The young count was also in the early stages of growing a beard which enhanced his features, that included a straight aristocratic nose, full lips, and an oval face. He wore a black vest over a long white shirt without a collar and black-and-white checkered trousers.

"This is Carmen. She is our happiest *margouin*," he added, referring to the model. His large, dark eyes sparkled with mischief. "We all love when she works with us. She's a vision." The woman smiled as she nodded and tightened the sash of her robe.

"*Enchante*, Mademoiselle Carmen," Theo said as he bowed his head in greeting and turned to Lautrec. "Henri, this is my older brother, Vincent. He is a new student, just arriving from the north. I hope you will help him get acclimated to the teaching studios."

Vincent extended his hand, and the small man shook it enthusiastically, saying, "I am honored to welcome you to our little group, Vincent. I trust we are not too juvenile and frivolous for your taste."

Lautrec was referring to the obvious difference in age and background between Vincent and the other students in the atelier. Most of the artists were at least ten years younger than van Gogh and were high-spirited Frenchmen who enjoyed their art and their lifestyle. Most were from wealthy families that supported their art education and had affluent social lives.

Despite his youth and physical deformity, Henri was the *massier*, the accepted leader of the group. His aristocratic breeding and magnetic personality gave him access to many important people throughout Paris. Cormon expected him to control the other students in his absence with his powerful voice and sparkling conversation.

"Vincent, you're going to appreciate the world of Montmartre," Henri offered. "For a painter, it's a unique place to let your imagination run wild. It's a big zoological park, and you are the lion tamer."

The new immigrant from the north did not fully understand the metaphor. Nonetheless, the model's rest period was almost over. Van Gogh obtained a list of materials from one of the instructors, who told him where to purchase the required art supplies in the neighborhood. As they left the salon, Vincent and Theo bade the others farewell. They were pleased with their morning visit to Atelier Cormon.

6

Later that same day, Vincent walked from his brother's flat on Rue de Duval to Boulevard Montmartre. The rundown, working-class neighborhood gave way to an upscale, prosperous environment. He was heading toward his brother's art gallery in the center of Paris. Vincent looked like a different person from the one who had arrived on these streets only a day before.

Entering the gallery, he was approached by Leon, the sales associate. "Bonjour, monsieur, may I be of assistance?"

Vincent remembered all the times he had to greet new customers when he worked at Goupil's Gallery in Paris, in London, and, before that, at The Hague. "Oui, Leon, it is I, Vincent. I have come to see my brother."

"Oh! Monsieur van Gogh, please forgive me. I did not recognize you. Your brother is with a client, but I shall tell him you are here."

"*Merci*, Leon, I care to look at these paintings while I wait."

"Very well, monsieur," said Leon, retiring from the front room.

The artist was drawn to a large painting by Jean-Francois Millet showing three dignified farm workers tilling the soil by hand. As Vincent looked at the painting, another sales associate approached and began to apply a standard sales promotion. "Monsieur, you'll notice in this Millet the tautness of line combined with great delicacy and refinement in the handling of the paint. This depiction of the brutalized peasants is done with an uncompromising realism and provides a sentimental appeal to city dwellers."

Van Gogh looked away from the painting and right into the fellow's eyes. "What is your name, young man?"

"It is Paul."

"Well, Paul, what do you really feel about this painting?" Answering his own question, the artist continued, "It must speak to your spirit, to your soul. Paul, before you can sell a painting, you have to know how it motivates the human spirit, and you must start with your own."

The boy knew he was in over his head. "Pardon! Monsieur, you must be a painter, *non*?"

"Oui, art is my personal spiritual redemption. It releases my violent, frustrated passions. And Paul, always remember that painting peasants is very serious business."

At this point, the young salesman became apprehensive and started to back away.

The Dutchman made the tense situation worse by letting out a thunderous laugh. "I banter with you, my boy, having occupied your position ten years ago. The directeur is my brother, and I wait to see him."

The young man was partially relieved and through a half-smile responded, "Very well, monsieur, I leave you to look at the other paintings." He turned and quickly left the artist alone in the front room.

Van Gogh was interested in a landscape of the Italian Volterra by the Barbizon artist Jean-Baptiste Corot. As he looked at the ornate, golden frame around the large painting, his mind returned to his time at the gallery in London.

He held the door for the day's last customer. "Good-bye, sir. We hope to be of service upon your return to Goupil's Gallery of London." Vincent locked the door and began to straighten up the gallery and his desk in preparation for the following day.

The younger Vincent van Gogh was athletic and muscular with long curly hair and a cheerful disposition. He jumped when he heard a sharp tap on the front window. Vincent looked up and saw a charming blonde with sparkling white teeth. From the sidewalk, she looked at him and appeared anxious.

A smile came to his face as he waved and held up his finger to tell her to wait a minute and that he would be there momentarily. He strode back to the manager's office. "Mr. Obach, I have closed the gallery. Sir, may I leave for the day?"

The manager was reviewing some invoices and without looking up responded, "Why certainly, Mr. van Gogh. You may go. We shall see you in the morning."

As Vincent got out to the street, Eugenia ran over and took his hand in hers for the walk to the boardinghouse. Vincent had been a boarder in Eugenia's mother's home for the past three months and had fallen in love with the pretty nineteen-year-old woman. It highlighted the young man's twentieth summer and had made it the best summer of his life so far.

"I never thought the day would end," he said. "I have been thinking about you, my love, since this morning."

Eugenia squeezed his hand and looked into his eyes. "Let's not go home. My mother and Uncle Kenneth are there. We've been arguing all afternoon. It's a beautiful summer's evening. Perhaps we could walk through the park?"

As the young couple entered Hyde Park, they followed a walkway that led to a hill overlooking a small pond. On the hill, they stopped. Vincent took her in his arms and kissed her. "Jean, you are so important to me. Have you thought about what we discussed last night?"

"Oh, Vincent, I don't know. It's a lot more complicated. I have to consider my family's concerns."

"Jean, I love you. When we are together, I know you cannot bear to let me go. We should marry and have a family."

Vincent sat on the grass, and Eugenia sat down next to him. It was very quiet, and the busy city appeared miles away. Van Gogh kissed the young woman's lips and put his hand into her blouse, caressing her breasts with his eager touch.

Taking hold of his hand, Eugenia said, "Please, I must discuss a matter of importance."

"What's wrong? What's happened?" Vincent asked.

Eugenia covered herself and straightened her clothing. "Remember when I said mother and I have been arguing?"

"What did you discuss?"

"It is difficult for me to find the words ... but I just cannot marry you. My mother and my entire family want me to wed Mr. Malcom Berkley, the town-house developer."

"Berkley? That pompous braggart who comes to have dinner with your mother? He is old enough to be your father."

"My mother has forbidden me to marry you. Moreover, Uncle Kenneth has already informed Mr. Berkley he may have my hand."

"Eugenia, what does your uncle have to do with our lives?"

"He's like a father to me and has some serious reservations about your financial ability to support marriage at this time. Vincent, my dear, we cannot be together again."

The distraught young man walked Eugenia home to the boardinghouse in complete silence. When the couple entered the building, Eugenia's relatives would not speak to Vincent. Devastated, Vincent went to his room and took to his bed for three days, sending word to the gallery that he was sick with influenza.

When he did return to his duties, van Gogh lost interest in his position, becoming impolite and abrupt with the customers. Mr. Obach had him transferred to the Paris gallery, where he was dismissed from the company a short time later.

"Vincent, I'm sorry to have left you alone," Theo said. "I was busy in my office with a client."

Vincent came back from his thoughts about London and Eugenia and looked at his brother. "Ah, Theo! I just stopped in to look at those Impressionist paintings you have been telling me about. I see Corot, Millet, and Daumier, all classical artists. Where are the avant-garde?"

"Not too loud. Monsieur Boussod has instructed me to keep them on the mezzanine for special customers who are looking for Impressionist and modern paintings."

"Well, lead the way to the secret stash of impressions."

Theo led him up the side stairs to the mezzanine, which was well lit by natural light from a large skylight. On the walls were seven paintings: two by Monet, two by Degas, and one each by Renoir, Cézanne, and Pissarro. There were also about twenty-five paintings on artists' racks under the paintings.

Vincent started to examine the canvases. He was mesmerized by the luminous colors and brief strokes and dabs. He had never seen painting like it. "*Dieu damne*, Theo, I have never imagined they would look like this. The subjects are from everyday life but are full of atmosphere."

Theo folded his arms across his chest. "Most of these paintings have been done *sur le motiv*, in the open."

"Yes, but the lack of draftsmanship has given rise to bright, pure color used to illustrate the passing effects of light," said Vincent. "It's a protest against the dusty studio art of the Salon."

"So, my older brother, you are in favor of the Impressionists?"

"Oh, Theo, a picture is surely worth a thousand words. Everything you wrote and told me about these canvases does not compare to seeing them in the flesh. I feel that I have wasted the last years of my life. My work is so dark and drab next to these jewels of light. Everything I've done is hopelessly out-of-date. I want to go back to the flat and throw my canvases in the fire."

"No, Vincent, you are a talented artist who will emerge with your own artistic idiom. The dark, somber, tonal quality of the Dutch masters is the best grounding a modern artist can have. Use what you have learned to go on and paint what is inside of you."

Leon, the sales associate, interrupted the brothers' art discussion. "Monsieur van Gogh, Monsieur Pissarro is here to see you."

"Excellent, Leon. Show him up to the mezzanine."

"This is most fortunate. Pissarro is one of the best Impressionists with a solid grounding in the academics."

When he entered the room, Pissarro's height overwhelmed Vincent. He was in his late fifties with a large head and a full gray beard.

After the introductions, Theo told the older artist that Vincent was quite taken with Impressionism. He also mentioned that his brother was about to start at Cormon's atelier.

"Well, my good man, you have entered a war zone."

"I have, monsieur?" asked Vincent. "What do you mean by that?"

"Not a war separating armies, but a conflict between two schools of thought about art. Even though the Impressionists' movement is twelve years old, established art circles still view this genre as an illegitimate stepson of academic art."

"But Theo exhibits you Impressionists in this gallery. Surely, there must be a market for the avant-garde?"

Theo interrupted in a low, quiet voice. "Well, my employer, Monsieur Boussad has warned me that placing an Impressionist work in the gallery's front window could cause a major street disturbance, possibly a riot."

"Most bourgeois," added Pissarro, "especially middle-class connoisseurs, despise Impressionism and doubt the intrinsic value of our paintings."

"What about the younger artists and the students?" asked Vincent.

"I have found that most of the young are totally captivated by Impressionism. But you should know that your new teacher, Fernand Cormon, is a conservative, academic painter who opposes our movement. He favors romantic compositions in the grand traditions of the past—historical subject matter with moralizing themes."

"His most famous painting, *The Family of Cane Escaping*, was based on the Old Testament narrative," added Theo. "It was executed with natural skin tones and possesses an almost photographic quality."

"Speaking of photography," said Vincent, "why is the public so fascinated with this new invention. Will it replace painting?"

"No," answered Pissarro. "I believe that photography actually promotes Impressionism. It shows that art is more than a detailed duplication of a physical scene."

"So, in other words," said Vincent, "a camera's image is very static, lacking mood and emotion. It's up to the artist to imbue his work with his own perspective and impressions that go beyond the physical scene."

"Your brother is very perceptive, Theo. He'll go far in this crazy profession. I thank you for your time. I just stopped by to inquire if any of my paintings have sold recently."

"Well, we sold one last month, as you know," said Theo, "but this month is still young."

"Thank you, Theo. You do a fine job here at Boussod & Valadon. I just wish we could put some of my paintings in the front window."

The men laughed. Camille Pissarro bowed and left the mezzanine.

Vincent turned toward his brother and said, "I want to learn to paint like these Impressionists."

"Yes, but in your own style. I know all of these painters," responded Theo. "I want you to meet with them and talk to them about their techniques. But you should select or reject those principles, as they conform with your own personal vision."

7

As Vincent and Theo discussed Impressionism, a little drama was unfolding across town. Suzanne Valadon, an eager and cheerful model, climbed the stairs to reach Henri's studio. She had posed in the studio five times in the last two weeks, and the painting was nearing completion.

After knocking, she could hear the harsh taps of a cane hitting the hardwood floor as Lautrec came to the door. It swung open, and there stood Henri in a clean gray smock that fit loosely over his white shirt and trousers. The little count's eyes were filled with admiration for the strikingly beautiful woman who stood before him.

He took her hand and kissed it gently, saying, "Suzanne, I am delighted to see you again. Please, come in out of the cold."

Afternoon light cascaded down the walls of the room from huge, glass sky-lights. In the center of the studio, an ambient glow illuminated the platform that held an off-white chaise lounge near a small table.

The walls were virtually hidden by stacked canvases, large picture frames, and piles of drawings and photographs. Mounds of bric-a-brac were scattered around the room. They included items the artist sentimentally treasured, such as metal toys for children, military accoutrement, Japanese ceramics, and antique clocks.

Henri took the young woman's coat and hung it on the wall near a variety of hats, shawls, dressing gowns, and other forms of apparel. Lautrec grabbed a cloche, a woman's bell-shaped hat, and put it on his head. He started dancing around, imitating a Parisian chanteuse with a falsetto voice.

"You sound like a little girl," Suzanne responded as she broke into a hearty laugh and began to join in the singing.

He spun her around in a slow circle as they laughed together. All the while, the little count watched her through his pince-nez with his big eyes as if he wanted to permanently commit the scene to his memory.

The woman broke from his gaze and went back to the wall, where she removed an elaborately decorated satin robe from a hook. "Should I wear the kimono again today, Monsieur Henri?"

"Oui, my dear. We are almost finished with this painting. It's been going very well."

Lautrec went over to a high table in the corner of the room and began to uncork a bottle of wine. Without a word, Suzanne moved to a small divan near the clothing wall. She quickly removed all of her clothes and placed them on the divan. Very carefully, she slid the kimono over her shoulders without placing her arms into the sleeves. She did not fasten the garment but enwrapped it loosely around her décolletage.

"Suzanne, I have some superb wine from the eastern Rhône, which I hope you will approve of." As he spoke, Henri tried not to watch the woman undressing, but he followed her in the corner of his eye. He poured some Beaujolais into two wine glasses. He brought one glass to the small metal table, which also held a lighted glass lamp, near the chaise. The white-yellow light of the lamp bathed one side of the chaise in a warm glow. He placed the other wine glass on a little shelf attached to the large easel about five steps in front of the platform.

After picking up his palette, Lautrec started to mix and replenish some of the paints, which had dried since the last time he had worked on the canvas. As he prepared his palette and brushes, Suzanne walked in her bare feet across the floor, picked up her wine glass, and sat down on the chaise lounge.

Lautrec looked at the canvas. "Suzanne, please assume the position from the last session."

Suzanne sat back on the sloping part of the chaise with her graceful body following the natural curve of the lounge. She opened the kimono from her smooth throat to below the rounded cleavage of her breasts. The model held the shiny garment closed in her lap. Her bare legs were crossed above the ankle, with her toes pointing downward.

The room became very quiet. When Suzanne looked up in the direction of the easel, she saw a grotesque face encircled in red horns moving toward her. She jumped back and almost fell off the chaise. Henri was wearing one of his newest possessions, an antique battle helmet from the Far East.

"Don't be afraid. It's only me, Yuo Ichi of Yokimoto."

"What is that? That's the strangest hat I have ever seen!" said the startled woman holding her chest.

"Do you like my new samurai helmet from eighteenth-century *Japon*?" said Lautrec like a little boy enjoying a new toy. "The samurai were the warriors, the last great individuals of our age. They have all been defeated by the Meiji rulers of the new empire of Japon."

Suzanne responded, "Is that why art and wood-block prints from Japon are all the rage among the artists of the Petite Boulevard?"

"Partly, my dear, for the new rulers of Japon have finally opened up their society to trade and Westerners," answered Lautrec.

"Well, I think you look very debonair in your new hat," replied Suzanne. "Let's drink a toast to the gallant samurai."

As she raised her glass, the kimono slipped from her shoulders, exposing her smooth shoulders and full breasts with their tawny pink nipples. Henri took off the helmet, drank the rest of his wine, and walked slowly toward Suzanne without his cane. He sat down next to her on the lounge, took her face in his hands, and kissed her gently on the mouth.

He took the kimono from around her body, removed his smock, and lay down beside her. After kissing Suzanne on her face and eyes, he moved down her neck, finally placing his open mouth on her breasts. He could hear a guttural sound within her breath as he unbuttoned his trousers and freed his excited organ. Henri placed her hand on his penis.

"Please enter me, Henri. I desire you within me," she pleaded.

"Ah, Suzanne, my darling, I want you to enjoy every moment."

As the skillful lover forced his erection deep inside her, she yielded a lusty moan. Suzanne responded to his every move until they both collapsed in a rapture of shared ecstasy.

As they looked up at the overhead skylights, the light of day was almost gone. The lamp near the chaise provided the only illumination on their bodies, still aglow from their lovemaking.

"That was a marvelous turn of events, my dear," he said, placing the discarded artist's smock over the lower part of his body. "It appears we have not progressed very much with the painting."

"You know, I took your advice and have started to paint. I just love the colorful movement of nature, and my art communicates that love."

"I have not seen your painting, but I can attest that you certainly know how to communicate love."

They both laughed as he put his arms around her, and she moved closer.

"Suzanne, I know you have had a difficult life. How do maintain your enthusiasm?"

"Well, my mother was an unmarried, poor laundress when I came along. We lived in the most run-down sections of Paris and I always had odd jobs just to survive."

"What job did you like the most?"

"When I was fourteen I learned to ride galloping horses around the circus ring."

"Amazing my dear, you were a performer in the circus?"

"Yes, I had perfected a trick where I jumped from the back of one running horse to another. Unfortunately, one evening, in front of a full house, I slipped and fell, seriously injuring my back. My career in the circus was over."

"What did you do next?"

"Old Mama had this idea that I get to know successful painters and gentlemen. She heard about the Sunday afternoon spectacle at Place Pigalle, where young, future muses line up to be selected by artists in need of inexpensive models."

"Oh yes, me and my colleagues have selected young models from Place Pigalle on Sunday afternoon."

"I remember that later in the afternoon we models were replaced by the working ladies of the evening, who detested sharing the square and its fountain with us innocent girls."

"Yes, Suzanne, the working girls have to protect their turf."

"But my innocence did not last long. There was this young painter, Boissy was his name. He told me he wanted to paint me on a continuing basis, and after a few late-night modeling sessions, he made love to me."

"How old were you by then?"

"I was eighteen and it was my first love affair, but Boissy started to lose interest in art, as well as love. When I found that I was pregnant, he was gone and I never saw him again. My son, Maurice, was born on Christmas Day, 1883."

"How did the experience change you? You do not seem bitter."

"No, Henri, the experience made me realize what I had to do to succeed in life. I had charm and beauty and knew how to use them. Within two years, I had become a favorite margouin and paramour of well-established artists, such as Pierre Puvis de Chavannes, Pierre-Auguste Renoir, and Edgar Degas."

"And now you are the favorite of Henri deToulouse-Lautrec Monfa."

They both smiled as Henri pulled Suzanne toward him and they resumed their intimacy.

8

Following Theo's directions, Vincent found Julien Tanguy's store of painting supplies on Rue Clauzel. Julien was a friendly old man, but he was suspicious of strangers. "May I be of service?" he said, rising from his workbench.

"Ah, you are new to the area, monsieur?"

Van Gogh looked at the lines of the old man's red face and his hesitant smile and knew immediately he would someday paint his portrait.

"Oui, I am new to Montmartre, a painter starting at Atelier Cormon. I was told you prepare the best oils in Paris."

"Where are you from? I detect you are not *français?*"

"Oui, I am from *la Hollande.*"

Tanguy seemed relieved that the visitor was not French. It gave him the opportunity to relive the most significant time in his life. He started to recount the history of Montmartre and how it was placed under federal control after the Commune Riots of 1871. "Oui, it was an impetuous rebellion, just when the invading Prussians came to occupy Paris. The people here, led by the students, wanted freedom from the central government. They were joined by our National Guard troops. Together, they captured all the cannons placed on La Buttes for defense of Paris."

Vincent interrupted. "But didn't they execute some French army generals in cold blood?"

Tanguy got a suspicious look on his face again and wondered if he had said too much to this outsider. "No, *le trouble* had been over for more than fifteen years," he thought. "People no longer cared." Finally, he blurted out, "The French Army *Regulier* killed twenty-five thousand in one terrible week."

The artist got an incredulous look on his face. "Monsieur Tanguy, I visited Paris five years later, and I was not aware of such a tragedy."

The old man's face turned almost purple. "Dutchman, the bourgeois didn't want you to know! At the time, the French newspapers said it was impossible to estimate the number killed on both sides."

To calm the shopkeeper, van Gogh interjected, "Oh yes, I agree. Newspapers try to avoid the truth when they might offend those in power. They take the side of the bourgeoisie."

Just then, Madame Tanguy, a short and stocky matron, appeared from the living quarters in the back of the shop and also attempted to calm her husband. "*Père*, father, leave the poor artist alone. No more *politique*. He just wants to purchase some supplies."

But like a dog with a bone, Tanguy did not drop the subject. "Let me just say, my new artist friend, that three blocks from where we are standing, at Place de Clichy, three hundred people were bayoneted to death in thirty minutes by the troops. Many more innocent people ran to the fields and cemeteries at the top of the butte, but they were hunted down and killed."

Vincent had learned about the Commune riots and the Franco-Prussian War when he visited in Paris in the 1870s. He did not realize that it was so devastating to the people of Montmartre. Tanguy's description was both chilling and fascinating. Van Gogh found out later that Tanguy and members of his family spent years in prison after the suicidal Commune riots when Parisians were killed by their own countrymen.

The Dutchman purchased a number of paint colors from Tanguy, including Naples yellow, cadmium orange, viridian green, alizarin crimson, and cobalt blue. These colors were included on his list of required materials for Cormon's atelier. They were also colors that were absent from Vincent's paint box because he hardly ever used them. Painting on his own, he had been drawn mostly to earth tones and darker, somber colors. He also purchased brushes and other art materials.

Madame Tanguy calculated the cost of the supplies. She received the corresponding francs as payment from van Gogh and deposited them in her apron.

Julien held out his large, rough hand in a firm handshake and said, "I thank you for your business and your patience with an old man babbling on about the *politique*."

"No, monsieur, it is compelling the way you speak from the heart. I know you are a man of the people. I can relate to injustice and suffering, thinking of myself as an artist of the poor and the downtrodden."

"And I know you are a good painter. When you finish your first canvases at Cormon's, you will bring them to me. If they are good, I'll put them in the window and sell them for you."

Madame Tanguy lifted her eyes to heaven and, clasping her hands together, let out a woeful sigh. Vincent tried not to notice. "Merci, monsieur. I am grateful for your confidence, and I will be back. Adieu, Madame Tanguy."

As the painter left the shop and strode up the street, he looked at Montmartre in an entirely new light. He understood why it was still considered a no-man's-land, a refuge for shady characters and criminals. Van Gogh remembered that when he lived in Paris during the 1870s, police looked at many of the people of La Buttes with suspicion and were wary of the gangs of young ruffians who inhabited the area. Some were called *apaches*. They roamed the streets in packs and wore wide berets, woolen sweaters, and corduroy pants. They could be trouble, especially at night.

Respectable women did not go out alone at night. The less respectable were around night and day as prostitution had been legal and regulated in France since Louis XIV. In Montmartre, enforcement of the laws regulating vice were arbitrary and spotty compared with the rest of Paris. For two francs, a man here could employ a prostitute, a *poule*, to satisfy his desires.

As much of Paris was going through a *siècle deslumieres*, or enlightenment, there were many impoverished people who could only afford to live in Montmartre. As in any metropolis of its time, the poor inhabitants, including many unemployed and destitute, could barely survive. On the positive side, the rent in Montmartre was relatively cheap, and the light and air quality was better than in downtown Paris. Furthermore, the atmosphere bubbled with uninhibited freedom.

Montmartre was actually two different realities within one urban village. The escarpment of La Buttes dominated the northern side of the city. The streets around the side and lower parts of La Buttes were quite developed and urbanized. The higher a person climbed up the escarpment, the more remote and rustic Montmartre became. Vegetable gardens, fields, and windmills dotted the top of the hill. Beyond the hill, a section of ramshackle houses called the maquis was home to the truly indigent, including members of street gangs and prostitutes.

As more writers, painters, entertainers, and their *associetes* moved into Montmartre, the area became more gentrified and more a venue of local entertainment. Enterprising entrepreneurs began to open bistros, cabarets, and inns to attract the pleasure-seekers of Paris. Some old mills and warehouses were being converted to dance halls and *café-concerts*.

9

The teaching ateliers were the contemporary equivalent of the academies that dated back to the Italian Renaissance. The early artists of Florence and Rome, eager to show they were cultured professionals and not mere craftsmen, organized academies as alternatives to the medieval guilds.

Later, art academies sprang up throughout Europe. By far, the most famous and powerful, however, was France's Royal Academy of Painting and Sculpture, organized in 1648. Under the protection of the king's minister, only the academy could hire models for life drawings or hold public exhibitions. Like academies elsewhere, the French Royal Academy set up training programs and scholarships for young artists, promoted strict standards of artistic quality, and organized official exhibitions—the most important being the annual Salon held in the Louvre Palace in Paris.

In Paris in the 1880s, an academic artist who was accepted by the Salon could very well become a financially successful painter. Critically acclaimed paintings sold for hundreds of thousands of francs at a time when the average working man earned a few francs per day. The fate of artists rejected by the Salon was often oblivion and difficulty earning an independent living.

Claude Monet, together with Edgar Degas, Pierre-Auguste Renoir, Alfred Sisley, Ms. Berthe Morisot, Camille Pissarro, and twenty-five other artists, held the first Impressionist Exhibition in 1874 at the studio of their photographer-friend Nadar. These artists were dissatisfied with their dependence upon the selection jury of the official Salon for their success. But critics lashed out at the new approach, calling it arrogant and revolutionary. They were horrified at the modern subject matter, the unfinished quality of the work painted out in the open, and the lack of draftsmanship. The term "Impressionism" was coined by an unfriendly critic, Louis Leroy, when he saw a painting by Claude Monet called *Impression: Sunrise*, which showed a view of the port of Le Havre painted in the mist.

The Impressionists, unlike the academic painters, tended to paint *en plein aire*, recording the changing conditions of light and atmosphere as well as their individual sensations in nature. They used high-key palettes and different kinds of brushstrokes that allowed them to express the impact of light on surfaces.

10

At his first morning at Cormon's, Vincent arranged his new supplies on his drawing station as the other students began to arrive. Though early in the morning—it was not yet 7:30—the young men were animated and talkative as they filtered into the rooms of the atelier.

"Bonjour, monsieur. Today is your first day?"

Van Gogh turned to see a smiling young man sitting at the next table. Being inherently self-conscious, the Dutchman felt like an old relic alongside these smooth-skinned juveniles. Furthermore, strangers usually refrained from starting conversations with Vincent due to his remote and unusual manner.

The congenial young man continued. "My name is Emile Bernard. Did not I see you several days ago as you visited with another gentleman?"

"Oui, Emile. My name is Vincent. I was indeed accompanied by my brother Theo, and it is my first day at this studio."

Emile Bernard was only eighteen years old when he met van Gogh in Cormon's atelier. Born in Lille, he had come to Paris at age ten with his family. His father wanted him to join the family business, manufacturing and selling cloth. But the young man wanted to become an artist and enrolled in the Ecole des Arts Décoratifs in his early teens.

He was tall and thin with a clean-shaven face. His dark hair was neatly combed, and he was dressed in a brown three-piece suit, the attire of the progeny of a well-to-do bourgeois family.

"I am also a new arrival at Cormon's, starting last month," said Bernard as he removed his suit jacket and replaced it with an artist's smock.

"I imagine that makes you the seasoned veteran in this part of the atelier."

With an amiable laugh, the young artist offered, "You will enjoy the studio. It's quite lively, the consequence of very little formal instruction."

Showing a touch of disappointment, Vincent asked, "So Cormon does not lecture or teach the academic fundamentals?"

"Oh, no, Fernand will watch over your work with very little criticism. He's a very conservative artist, but he lets each student pursue his own style."

"But aren't you looking for the structure of formal courses?"

"Monsieur, most artists here passed the academic stage of their development long ago. I myself was grounded in the academic principles by the time I was sixteen."

Vincent discerned that he was out of his element. He had been drawing for ten years, but only painting seriously for less than five. Most of his art education had been self-taught. He had acquired skills through reading, experimenting, and visiting museums in Amsterdam, London, The Hague, and Antwerp. However, his abiding interest in art could be traced to his mother, Anna Cornelia, who taught him the essentials of drawing at an early age.

Van Gogh was still searching for his own style, a genre that satisfactorily expressed his dramatic emotions and unique observations. In his previous paintings, Vincent chose subjects similar to those of the old Dutch masters Rembrandt, Hals, and Vermeer. He initially experimented with their techniques by studying their work at the Rijksmuseum in Amsterdam and by reading art books. However, being both perceptive and objective, he was frustrated when his own renditions did not exhibit the superior skills emanating from the old masters' works.

Even though Vincent's formal academic education was limited, he did possess an acutely analytical mind coupled with a compulsive drive. The result was an accumulation of a complex body of knowledge of formal art topics covering drawing, tonal quality, perspective, and art appreciation that spanned four centuries.

In fact, when it came to art, the Dutchman was a walking encyclopedia. However, his low self-esteem and lack of social grace made him feel insecure around better educated, sophisticated artists.

A thin, fastidious man walked into the section of the salon where Emile and Vincent sat. Gaston, the atelier's studio manager, looked like a smaller, thinner version of his superior, Fernand Cormon. He arranged for the models and directed the activities taking place during the hours of operation.

Following him at a short distance was a shabbily dressed little boy about eight years of age. "Gentlemen, this is Pierre, today's margouin. I am going to seat him in this little chair here on the platform. Please use your graphite crayon and your charcoal with a large-sized, medium-weight paper for this morning's exercise."

Gaston abruptly left the platform and walked into the atelier's other salon to work with the oil painters on their morning assignments. In addition to Bernard and van Gogh, only four other artists were engaged in drawing the portrait of the young boy. The group hurriedly began sketching their subject, starting with the considerations of general shape and placement.

Van Gogh looked at Pierre, trying to read the life in the little fellow's eyes. He wondered how the child came to this type of work. Did he have parents living? Did he ever attend school? A million questions raced through his mind. Normally, he tried to spend time with his models, learning about their individual struggles for life. Often, he acted more like a sociologist than a painter.

After about five minutes, Vincent had not even put down the first mark on his sketching paper. His face took on the detached look of a man in a trance, hypnotized by the scene.

Suddenly, Vincent picked up the crayon and charcoal and, without looking down at the paper, started to furiously cover the surface with scattered marks and smudges. Constantly using a mark eraser and his finger, he mitigated and blended the graphite and charcoal lines. After another ten minutes, van Gogh was finished with the drawing. He put down his implements and folded his arms over his chest.

Every one of the other artists, including Bernard, was still in the beginning phases of his drawing. Vincent could not decide if he was content or dissatisfied by his efforts. He sat quietly looking at his drawing and back at the boy.

Van Gogh then turned the paper over and started to draw even faster on the other side of the parchment, starting the drawing over right from the beginning. Fingers, arms, and elbows again moved at lightning speed across the illustration.

Vincent worked on his drawing for about the same amount of time as the first and upon finishing felt quite satisfied. He spent the rest of the session doing small drawings of the child's hands, his face, and especially his worn out shoes.

After about an hour, the little model could hardly sit still any longer. Gaston told Pierre to take a rest and directed him to the water closet. He would pose differently later with the oil painters in the other salon, standing in his long overcoat and holding a child's toy gun.

Bernard came over to van Gogh's table and asked, "How did you like today's first drawing exercise?"

"The boy is an excellent subject, but I hope Gaston is paying him a decent wage for this work. The poor little fellow looks like he's never had a childhood and never will."

"He's probably a *poulbot*, a fearless little urchin of the maquis," added Emile, "an offspring of the vagabonds who live in those wooden shacks up over the butte." Without being obvious, he glanced at Vincent's drawing. It looked nothing like a line drawing but an early Dutch painting with harsh shadows and shadings throughout for dramatic emphasis in various tonal shades of gray, brown, and off-white paint. Down the side of the boy's little face, Vincent had added silver, sorrowful tears where no tears had been visible. Pierre looked like a miniature version of an old man.

For the rest of the day, the artists of the drawing section practiced with still life of plaster casts of various body parts. Vincent's treatment was predictable and his results outstanding. Even Gaston, who normally only criticized drawings, avoided saying much about van Gogh's work. It was obvious that Vincent was an outstanding illustrator, but the instructor was not in the habit of giving a compliment to a beginning student.

Professeur Cormon stopped by after spending time with the oil painters in the other room. He looked at Vincent's drawings and also reserved comment, except in a general way. "I see you are getting along well in our little school."

"Oui, monsieur le professeur, but when do I embark upon the oil painting?"

"There's plenty of time for that, Vincent. I would like you to remember that an artist can never draw well enough. To become a great painter, one should draw everyday, even if it is just a little sketch."

With that, Cormon moved over to the other artists' stations. He glanced at their illustrations and then turned and left the room.

The session lasted until one o'clock. Afterward, some students remained at the atelier to work on projects, while others left for the day. Many went to their own studios, and others painted *en plein aire* at various locations around Paris. Some were assigned to go to the Louvre to paint a replica of a famous masterpiece that hung in the museum's salons.

Vincent was about to leave when he heard Monsieur Henri's thunderous voice approaching from the other salon.

As he walked into the room, Lautrec recognized Emile and Vincent sitting at their tables. "How are the new illustrators doing? This is the honorable work; it's the only way to learn to do portraits."

Bernard responded, "Monsieur Henri, there is more to art than just portraits. Not everyone is fascinated exclusively with personalities."

"Bernard, let's not proceed with this debate again. You Impressionists put too much into landscape. Nothing exists but the figure. Landscape is nothing, and should be nothing. It's only an accessory, and a painter who paints pure landscape is an idiot."

Vincent also disagreed with Henri. "How do you rationalize Courbet, Corot, or Delacroix? Surely, their landscapes are indeed masterpieces."

The little count replied, "A good landscape is great when it is handled like a face. Gentlemen, this discussion could go on all day. Let the three of us adjourn to Le Tambourin for dinner tonight. It's right across the boulevard. And Vincent, ask your brother if he would care to join us."

The men agreed that they would meet at eight o'clock, and Vincent was most pleased. His acquaintances normally had no interest in his opinions on anything, especially art. Tonight, Vincent would have dinner with an aristocrat. Apparently, Paris had many surprises in store for him.

11

Vincent arrived at Café du Tambourin, an earthy cabaret on Boulevard de Clichy, with his preoccupied younger brother. Theo had seemed reluctant about accepting the dinner invitation and going out this evening.

As they approached the café, Theo finally admitted, "My former lover Agostina is Tambourin's owner. I should not be here tonight. She thinks we still have a connection."

"Ah, you waited all this time to tell me. You never discuss your personal life, Theo."

"But we are here now. What am I going to do?" Theo paused uncertainly outside the door.

"It's better to have a quarrel with an old mistress than to have a misunderstanding with a new one. I'm going in to have a nice dinner, and I suggest you do the same," Vincent replied.

After entering the bistro, they were jostled by the laughter and chatter of the rowdy customers standing around the bar. The brothers moved through the crowd to the front tables of the long, narrow restaurant. The motif was a curious mixture of gypsy and Italian with round tables gaily painted to resemble tambourines and with seats like cowhide drums. On the walls hung dusty, old, romantic paintings of Italy. The brothers tried to find Henri and Emile through the noise and cigarette smoke.

Le Tambourin was a lively representation of the eclectic nature of Montmartre. Around the bar were shabbily dressed men in faded black who looked like criminal cutthroats. They laughed loudly as they cajoled a pair of coarse but lighthearted ladies of the evening. White-collar bourgeois gentlemen spoke in hushed tones to their well-dressed ladies. Bohemian writers and artists arguing about their crafts filled the tables toward the back of the room. Waitresses in alluring Italian-peasant costumes dashed to and fro with giant trays filled with plates of food and drinks.

The brothers followed the loudest noise with their footsteps, which led through the smoke to the laughter of Monsieur Henri. He was holding court at a back corner table of the café. Beside Emile Bernard sat Louis Anquetin, another artist from Cormon's atelier whom everyone liked for his sense of humor, towering frame, and good looks.

Sitting with her back to the approaching men was a tall, dark-haired woman in a red and white blouse and a red skirt. Agostina, the proprietress, turned and looked at the two brothers.

Agostina Segatori was a former model in her late thirties who had posed for some of France's most celebrated contemporary artists. Since her early years, she had gained just a few pounds but still held an alluring figure and exotic Mediterranean features.

Her work with Jean-Baptiste Corot during his tour of Italy led her to immigrate to Paris's Montparnesse district. Known as *L' Italienne de Montparnesse*, Agostina continued to pose for the famous Barbizon painter who was nearly fifty years her senior. Despite the age difference, the two were very close, and when Père Corot died, his favorite model was despondent for many months. Subsequently, Agostina posed for the celebrated Jean-Leon Gerome, Eugene Delacroix, and Edouard Manet, among others.

For twelve years, she was the companion of the artist Edouard Dantan. The two had a son, Jean-Pierre, born in 1873. She and Dantan had separated before Agostina started the café. Little Jean-Pierre was raised by Agostina's mother and other members of the family who had also immigrated to Paris from Naples, Italy.

With her charming, stately manner, she was quite successful as a model and accumulated enough savings to open a café, first on Rue de Richelieu and later at 62 Boulevard de Clichy. Some say, she was also aided by an inheritance from Père Corot.

As *L' Italienne* focused on Theo, her warm brown eyes shrunk to little black stones, and her vivid red mouth dropped open.

Speaking in a quiet but firm tone, Theo began the conversation. "*Bonsoir*, Tina. *Comment allez-vous?* The café appears quite busy tonight."

"Where the hell have you been? I have not seen you for weeks. When I call at the gallery, they say you are not there."

"Tina, this is my older brother Vincent, an artist who has recently started at Cormon's studio across the boulevard."

"So, Vincent, are you just like your brother, a man who is too busy with his work to have time for a relationship with a woman?"

Vincent had no answer to the indictment, but he knew it was his turn to change the subject. Relying on a casual thought, he replied, "Well, Agostina, since arriving from the north, Theo's been very busy getting me settled. He's taken me to meet influential people in the art world. I'm sure he cares for you. After all, you are a beautiful woman."

Agostina realized this was not the time or place for confrontation. She stepped back and addressed the entire table. "What can we get you gentlemen from the kitchen? We have just made *saltimbocca alla Napoli*, and it is delicious."

Henri, who had been watching the little melodrama unfold, said, "Mademoiselle Segatori, it sounds exquisite. How is it made?"

"Veal *coquilles* wrapped in prosciutto with sage, just as they prepare the dish in Naples."

"That sounds delightful. Bring the veal for everyone." After looking around the table for any objections, Henri added, "And we require more *chianti classico*."

After Agostina retired to the kitchen, the new arrivals sat down with the other men. As usual, Henri was the first to speak. "Theo, I'm sorry I suggested this café tonight. It is always difficult to confront a former mistress. Tina is a voluptuous woman who obviously still cares for you. You could have done a lot worse."

Louis Anquetin quickly followed, "Oui, my friend, but once a woman has given you her heart, it's very hard to get rid of the rest of her."

The men laughed, and even Theo smiled meekly, not sure where the evening would take him. Agostina never came back to the table during the meal. The aged bottles of chianti were served by an enchanting waitress in a low-cut peasant blouse, who also brought the artists' antipasto, a first course of spaghetti, and the saltimbocca for the main course. After a dessert of assorted fruit and cheeses, Henri asked for some absinthe for the table.

The sommelier brought a small bottle of the emerald green liqueur, a large carafe of cool water, a plate of sugar cubes, a flat silver spoon with ornate holes cut along its broad face, and five empty glasses. Louis took one glass for himself and passed the other glasses around the table.

He picked up the bottle of absinthe and poured a small amount into the bottom of his glass. The silver spoon was placed on its broad face over the top of the glass. After placing a sugar cube on the spoon, he poured the cold water over the cube.

Vincent had tried absinthe before but had not ever witnessed this procedure, which seemed to take on a mystical significance. The sweetened water cascaded through the holes and mixed with the emerald absinthe, clouding up into a strange opalescence, an effect called the louche. Louis then passed the absinthe spoon to the next man sitting at the table.

As the other men prepared to enjoy an inexpensive high from this common drink of the day, they chose not to accept the mounting medical knowledge. Absinthe, also called *la fee verte*—the green fairy—was being linked to serious gastric disturbances, respiratory depression, kidney and liver failure, epileptic seizures, convulsions, madness, and suicide. In the Paris cafés of the day, the cocktail hour had become known as *l'heure verte*—the green hour. Absinthe was 72 percent alcohol by volume, 144 proof, a higher alcoholic concentration than rubbing alcohol. In addition to the alcohol, it contained a sizeable amount of insecticide made from the distillation of leaves and buds from wormwood, a herb used for centuries by many cultures in Europe and Asia to kill household worms, insects, and the parasites within the intestinal tract.

"Come on, Vincent. Your turn to get bitten by la fee verte," said Emile as he passed the silver spoon to the apprehensive artist.

"I've tasted absinthe before, but only in very small glasses. I'm not sure how much water to pour over the cube," protested van Gogh.

After drinking his absinthe, Theo gave his brother some advice. "You do not need much at all, just enough to turn the absinthe to a milky, cloudy color."

Vincent poured the water over the sugar and watched *la louche*. As he held the rim of the glass up to his face, the sharp, alcoholic vapors from the solution turned his head away. He had to close his eyes to take a small sip of the cloudy mixture, which tasted like bitter licorice mixed with inflammable lamp oil.

"That's not how you drink absinthe!" cried Lautrec. "You must drink it quickly, before your tongue has a chance to prevent you from swallowing. Do not breathe through your nose; just take a big gulp."

Vincent followed the instructions and took a mouthful, finishing almost all of the solution in his glass. His eyes and ears started to swell, and he could feel a burning all the way down his esophagus and the blood coursing through the vessels in the back of his head. The men around the table started to laugh at the humorous faces Vincent was making.

Henri held up his glass and said, "Let's have another round and a warm Montmartre welcome for Vincent van Gogh, our new artist from the north."

For the subsequent rounds of la fee verte, most of the drinkers did not use the spoon or sugar but just added water and absinthe without much ceremony. After four drinks of the green fairy, Vincent was physically unable to get out of his seat. Under the effects of mild euphoria, he was carried home to Rue de Laval by Louis and Theo, who supported him under his arms. When they put him to bed, he complained of vertigo and felt a hyperexcitability mixed with a strange lucidity. As he tried to sleep, he experienced mild hallucinations of bright, colorful lights.

He finally fell asleep and dreamed he was in a field early in the morning. As the sun came up, its color was not just red and yellow but also white, green, purple, and blue. In his dream, as he witnessed this strange sunrise, he composed an ode:

> *The opalescense of la fee verte bursts into the colors of my soul*
> *Awakening the legend that the rainbow is the sign of salvation.*
> *My peers are long dead, and even if I find companionship on earth,*
> *There are no twin souls in genius.*

Vincent had become friends with the green fairy, and the effect would be like a natural disaster, like an act of God that changes the course of a river. This friendship would become troubled and profound—both evil and productive—and last until the end of the artist's life.

12

"Rue Provence, *s'il vous plaît!*" exclaimed Henri as he and Vincent boarded the black cabriolet.

"Oui, monsieur, Le One-Two-Two of Madame Marcel," answered the cab driver as he cracked his whip in the crisp night air above the animal's rump. Vincent looked puzzled as the cab rumbled its way southward toward the elegant, grand boulevards of Paris. He and Henri wore the black derby hats and frock coats of smart Parisian gentlemen.

"Enjoy the journey, my friend," laughed Henri. "It's part of your initiation to Paris, which I'm certain you'll find fascinating."

"Where are you taking me?"

"We are going to the finest bordel in Paris."

In a steadfast canter, the carriage horse drew the cab through the dark, empty streets toward the *maison de tolerance* located at 122 Rue de Provence.

"It's known simply as Le One-Two-Two," said Henri. "This bordel has operated legally for many years."

"You French have no need to conceal your brothels. In Amsterdam, we keep them in one section of the city."

"We have a much more liberal view than you Dutch. Far from being concealed, brothels preserve family unity and act as a bulwark for bourgeois morality. Their intended purpose is the discouragement of divorce and homosexual behavior, control of venereal disease, and the maintenance of social order."

"Henri, you make it sound like getting laid is a public service." The men in the cab, including the driver, enjoyed a hearty laugh.

The black coach rolled to a controlled stop in a quiet street near an unassuming, four-story building with a smooth stone facade. Its ornately draped windows masked the flickering lights emanating from inside.

The silhouette of a man with a top hat graced the front entrance. His resonant voice pierced the darkness. "Bonsoir, Count Lautrec. I see you've brought a friend. Please have a pleasant evening, monsieur," he said, opening the door for the visitors.

As Vincent followed Henri through the entrance, a young woman in street attire asked politely for their hats and coats. Before handing over his coat, Henri removed a tablet from his pocket and a few charcoal pencils.

"Monsieur Henri, you have not been present for some time."

"Oui, Nicole, been working in my studio, but I'm here tonight. Where is Madame Marcel … and my Mireille?"

"La madame is occupied with investors in her office, but Mireille is here. Should I see if she is available?

"That is not necessary, straightaway. First, I'd like to show my friend around *la maison*."

"Of course, monsieur. You know la madame and *les dames de maison* treat you like family."

Vincent was intrigued. He had been to brothels before in other cities, but he had never been treated like a member of the family. It was unusual that Henri merited this degree of access in an establishment that essentially existed to provide clients with complete privacy in a milieu of discretion.

Henri led Vincent into the large parlor off the front foyer. Giant mirrors on the salon's walls reflected the pink and yellow light from the gas-fed crystal chandelier suspended from the ceiling. The room was half empty, with a few gentlemen sitting on rosewood furniture with red velvet upholstery and speaking quietly with several of the women. The ladies lounged dishabille—a casual state of being partially dressed—as if preparing to retire for the evening. Some wore frilly peignoirs over their *chemises de nuit*.

One young woman was dressed in a black chemise that only extended to the knee, emphasizing her shapely, crossed legs. Another wore a diaphanous bed gown over a pink negligee. Medium-healed pumps with black or white silk stockings were worn by all the women in the parlor.

The women not sitting with a gentleman greeted Lautrec with a smile. Some came over and greeted him with a kiss on each cheek, asking if he would sketch them this evening.

"This is my friend Vincent, also an artist, but much more serious. I want to show him the fabulous salons, starting with the tropical beach. Is it free currently?"

The young woman in the sleeveless chemise answered, "There is no one in the beach salon. I can take your artist friend up there, Monsieur Henri."

"No, that shan't be necessary, Gabrielle. I shall show him the room myself." Henri was uncharacteristically stern with the woman, and she went back to sitting by herself on the empty love seat.

"Let's go, Vincent. Out in the foyer is the staircase to the second floor. Those damned sloping stairs are difficult to negotiate."

As the men climbed the winding staircase, the little count held his cane and drawing materials in one hand and van Gogh's arm in the other.

"Henri, how is it possible to get to a beach by ascending stairs?"

"You'll see, my friend. In Paris, everything is possible."

The men approached a salon labeled La Mer Tropical. Lautrec took his cane, rapped loudly on the door, waited a few seconds, and walked inside. The room was unoccupied, but Vincent was amazed. The room held a deck overlooking an oceanfront beach. A small pool was incorporated into the floor of sand, and a mural depicted waves, water, clouds, and the horizon in the distance. Lounge chairs rested on the sand. Above the large Polynesian bed were native masks and spears. A few palm trees completed the scene.

"Gogh, is it not grand? Like a fantasy journey to a foreign land, and you can take a companion along."

A melodious voice sounded from the open door behind them. "Whom do you plan to take on your fantasy trip, Monsieur Henri?"

The men turned to see the smiling older woman who had posed the question. Madame Valtesse Marcel was the size of an over-stout opera singer, and she wore her gray hair in a neatly stacked bun on top of her head. Her large dress of brown silk, covered by a layer of sheer brown batiste, had a trim of Alençon lace on its neck and cuffs.

"Oh, *Tantine* Valtesse, you and I will take a real ship and leave Paris far behind."

"Count Henri, it is so good to see you. Did you tell your painter friend about our other pleasant escapes?"

Lautrec answered, "Let me recall, there's the Egyptian, Arabian, and, oh yes, the Roman salons."

"Henri, what about our sleeper-car salon that simulates a journey by rail? Another gives the illusion of traveling by ship, but the swaying bed might get you seasick."

"This is remarkable. Are all the Parisian *maisons* like this these days?"

Answering Vincent's question for Madame Marcel, Henri said, "No, many try to imitate Le One-Two-Two, but they cannot match Tantine's ability to create the illusion of love in a princely setting."

"What's the cost of this fantasy?" asked van Gogh.

"Fifteen francs," said the madame. "Oh yes, painters and soldiers get a discount. The experience for an artist would be eight francs plus gratuity."

"We painters are subsidized by the state," quipped Henri. "We're a national treasure."

Madame Marcel led the men in a quiet chuckle.

"I shall see you gentlemen later. I must go down to the front salon and serve as hostess to this evening's guests. Henri, if you want to sketch tonight, you will find fresh pastry and coffee in the girl's lounge."

After Madame Marcel left the artists, Henri brought van Gogh to the third floor. Walking down the corridor, Vincent could tell by the sounds and laughter that many of the rooms were occupied.

At the far end of the hallway, they came to a small lounge where several of les dames de maison were relaxing, smoking cigarettes and cigarillos, playing cards, and drinking coffee. A heat and cooking stove stood below the window toward the back of the room.

Henri was not in the least bit self-conscious. Walking into the lounge, he inquired, "How are you charming ladies this evening?"

The women greeted him with smiles and laughter.

"This is my friend, Vincent. He's also a painter."

"Is he here tonight to paint or to get laid?" said a self-assured, brown-eyed, beautiful young woman with brown curls, wearing a light blue peignoir. She was about nineteen and appeared to cherish her role as one of the most congenial and desirable cocottes in Le One-Two-Two.

"Mireille, you vixen, that's no way to greet a man who has traveled all the way from the Netherlands to be with us."

"Then he must be very tired. I'll put him to sleep on the train in the sleeper salon."

"Vincent, go with Mireille. She'll take good care of you. You'll go on a trip you won't soon forget."

"Henri? Didn't you come here tonight to be with Mireille?"

"No, I care to stay in the lounge and draw a few sketches. Maybe later, I'll decide to dip my paint brush."

Vincent cleared his throat nervously. "But, Henri, I ..."

Noticing Vincent's hesitation, Henri interjected, "Now, Vincent, do not be concerned about the money. Just go have a good time." Whispering so only Vincent could hear, he added, "There isn't another like her for satisfying a man."

Mireille took Vincent by the hand and, along with the heavy fragrance of her *Eau de Rose cologne*, guided him to a suite marked "Wagon Lit—Sleeping Car." Following the young woman into the salon, Vincent beheld a giant diorama of the French countryside, complete with farms and little towns in the distance.

On one side of the room, stairs led up to a railroad sleeper car. From the window of the sleeping compartment, the diorama attained a very realistic quality.

Mireille kicked off her slippers and lay on the bed. When Vincent put his weight on the mattress, he felt the entire bed swing, accentuating his movements. This made him feel like the faux car was swaying, as if a train was lurching over the rails.

"Aren't you going to take off your clothes, Monsieur Vincent?" said Mireille as she slipped out of her peignoir and slowly removed her chemise over her head, exposing her full breasts and curvaceous body. As Vincent undressed, she rose to her knees and lit a lamp on the bedside table. Still on her knees, she reached out and took Vincent's penis in both her hands. She stroked it, and as he became aroused, Mireille put his erection deep inside her mouth. She wet him thoroughly with her saliva and orally stimulated him for a few minutes before placing his excited organ into her vagina.

For almost an hour, Vincent enjoyed intense, uninhibited sex with the young woman. That was considerably longer than the typical experience at Le One-Two-Two. Mireille was well skilled in the techniques and positions of sex, and Vincent responded to her. She knew how to bestow the pleasure that a man desires.

"You are a most ardent and forceful lover, monsieur."

"Merci, my dear," answered the artist as he got dressed. "I can understand why you are Monsieur Henri's favorite in the maison. How long have you worked here?"

"I've been here about two years. I'm from Chambord in the Loire Valley."

"You cocottes are much the same as artists. We are both exiles, outcasts, but we enjoy a form of independence that is not without its advantages."

"Oui, and I'm very fortunate to have been selected to be a *fille de joie* in this bordel. The pay is good. I have my friends and many steady customers. And I can have all the food and clothing I need."

"How are the girls paid?"

"We get one half of the price, which madame puts into an account. Sorry to say, much of the money goes to pay our expenses. We keep the glove money, or the gratuity. In your case, Henri will pay Tantine, but if you could see your way to a little something …"

"Why of course, Mireille. Here, I have three francs. That's all I have with me."

"Merci, Monsieur! That's more glove money than I usually receive."

When Vincent got back to the lounge, Henri was deep in the drawing of two women lying on a couch in a corner of the lounge. Madeline, a red-headed woman in a chemise, was lying on her back while Satin, in a cotton camisole and fancy pantaloons, was lying nearby on her side, looking into her companion's eyes. They conversed as if Henri was not there. At times, one woman would touch the other's face or hair. They appeared to be more than platonic friends.

"Ah, the Dutchman has returned from his journey. Was Mireille to your liking?"

"Why, of course, she was splendid. But Henri, are these women posing? It looks very real to me."

"It is most certainly real life. Madeline and Satin mean the world to each other. And they are not the least bit self-conscious or prudish about it."

Lautrec then asked the women to walk across the hall into the Louis XV suite, which looked like a bedroom in the royal palace at Versailles. There, he urged them to take off their clothing and move on each other so he could capture their gliding movements.

"Gogh, don't these women look naturally naked? Their grace is reminiscent of the nymphs and goddesses of antiquity."

"I agree completely, Lautrec. Our professional models look clumsy in comparison."

"Gogh, close and lock the door. Let's give these nymphs a thorough screwing that is worthy of King Louis."

Van Gogh was both surprised and agreeable to the small man's proposal, and he guided the scarlet-haired Madeline to the giant Louis XV bed. Satin took Henri over to a chaise lounge covered in gold damask. The naked brunette sat before him and began to remove his clothing. When she unbuttoned his pants, the woman was confronted with an immense erection. "Oh, Monsieur Henri, I heard you were large, but this is *magnifique!*"

"Yes, my dear, I may be a small teapot, but I have a large spout."

Vincent let out a hearty laugh as he and Madeline sank into the soft down mattress of the giant bed. He thoroughly enjoyed his initiation to Le One-Two-Two, and the erotic session in the king's chamber lasted well into the night.

13

About a month had passed, and Vincent was becoming acclimated to the life of a Parisian art student. He and Emile had graduated to the oil-painting section.

Almost every evening, van Gogh made the rounds of the cafés and brasseries in Montmartre. Periodically, he would frequent Café du Tambourin just to see its charming proprietress, Agostina. Theo never accompanied Vincent to the Tambourin. His affair with the fiery Italian was indeed over, and he did not care to confront her. Vincent was attracted to the former model, but he always attended with a group so his interest would not become obvious. But whether at the Tambourin or any other café, van Gogh was always anxious to resume his close relationship with the green fairy. The artist became convinced that he could only sleep when under the influence of absinthe.

During the day, after Cormon's morning class, van Gogh would often wander his neighborhood, looking for scenes to paint. He liked to paint outdoor cafés and places where people congregated.

One afternoon, he and Emile were assigned by Gaston and Professeur Cormon to copy paintings by Eugene Delacroix at the Louvre. Loaded with easels and painting supplies, the two artists made their way to the museum's Salon Denon and the works of Delacroix.

"It's *The Girl with the Pearl Earring*, one of Vermeer's best portraits," said Emile as he and Vincent walked through the Dutch and Flemish Gallery.

"Oui, Johannes Vermeer has a timeless quality to his painting, but no one compares to Rembrandt," replied van Gogh. "Unfortunately, the Dutch painters do not invent; they have no imagination or fantasy."

Upon entering Salon Denon, van Gogh was the first to speak. "Bernard, see the way Delacroix paints? It's like a lion devouring its prey. He avoided lovemaking and never had serious love affairs so as not to waste the precious time that ought to be devoted to his work."

"What are you saying, Cent? You have to be a hermit or a priest to be a good artist?"

"No one enjoys sex more than me," replied van Gogh. "After all, the moment of coitus is a moment of infinity. But Balzac says comparative chastity only strengthens the modern artist. He claims painting and making love are not compatible. Sex saps the brain."

"Vincent, I think a man can go mad from too much sex or not enough."

"Well, if you put it that way, I would like to go mad from too much sex. Besides, I think I would prefer my own madness to the world's insanity."

Setting up their painting stations, the men chose two paintings side by side and began sketching the general forms with charcoal sticks. Van Gogh chose *Christ Asleep during the Tempest*, and Emile worked from *The Massacre of Chios*.

"I despise this assignment, copying work by another artist," said the Dutchman. "But I like the color Delacroix uses. The dark purple boat on a terrible emerald green sea is a brilliant use of complementary colors."

"Cent, I would much rather copy from an Impressionist, but Delacroix did know how to use color, and this is an excellent method for learning his technique. He knew how to use color, light, and movement to arouse emotion in his audience."

As the men worked on their paintings, visitors to the museum would periodically stand behind them to survey their progress. After about half an hour, a small crowd had gathered around Vincent's easel. The temperamental artist could stand it no longer. After picking up a clean palette from his supplies, he walked through the gathering and announced, "This is not a free show. If you want to watch our every move, it will cost you one franc each."

The little audience quickly scattered. "Bernard, I do not understand the French. I thought that we artists are national treasures?"

"Please be quiet, Gogh," whispered Emile from the side of his mouth. "Cormon will be furious if we get ourselves thrown out of the Louvre."

After refining their drawings, the artists blocked in the dark and light tones of their scenes with oil color. Next, they worked on the faces and small details of the paintings. Without realizing, the men had been working for nearly four hours without stopping for a break. Emile was the first to suggest that they adjourn and come back the next day.

Outside the museum, people were starting to leave the shops and offices on their way home. Many carried thin baguettes, traditional French bread eaten with the evening meal.

"Emile, let's get something to drink and eat. It's already the green hour."

Finding a nearby brasserie, the men stood at the bar and ordered some absinthe with glasses of beer and two beefsteak sandwiches.

"You know, Bernard, if one is to produce good work, one needs to eat well, to have one's fling from time to time, and to drink one's absinthe in peace. I do not care what Balzac thinks."

"I wish my father agreed with you," said the younger artist. "He has threatened to cut my allotment. He thinks my art is a foolish waste of effort, and that I must straightaway join the family business, manufacturing cloth for sale."

"Nonsense, I should have a word with your father."

"No thanks, monsieur, you and my father could never agree about anything. You are the prototype bohemian, and he is the bourgeois capitalist."

"Wouldn't your father agree that life is short, and we must spend it doing what we were intended to do?"

"Oui, but do we really know what we were intended to do?"

"Bernard, what about intuition? Even though scientists have proven that the earth is round and not flat, people still view life in a flat progression from birth to death. But scientists in the future will find that life is probably round and much more round than the world as we now know it."

"Now, you are a philosopher. I thought you were an artist?"

"Since moving to Paris, I've been contemplating many things. Before, I suffered from self-imposed isolation; today, I want to expand my world. I need a woman in my life."

"Does this woman have a name?"

"Yes, it's Agostina, from the café. I doubt that the feeling is mutual, but I feel like I've broken the prison of my loneliness. Without another person, one stays dead. Wherever affection is revived, there life endures."

"Cent, that woman does not even know you exist. When we go to her café, you are very formal and talk about the weather. And Agostina, she's a tough woman who is trying to run her own business."

"Oui, I realized that. But reaching out to another is the only way I can grow as a human being and an artist. When I look at the paintings of the modern artists, I see wonderful ways of expressing the art inside me. The difficult part is incorporating their techniques into my painting while still maintaining my own distinct style and principles."

14

In the evenings, van Gogh and his fellow students frequented the various brasseries along Boulevard de Clichy, which they called *le Petit Boulevard* because it ran through the Montmartre neighborhood of the younger, still-unsuccessful artists. The grand boulevards of downtown Paris were home to the established, celebrated artists such as Claude Monet, Auguste Renoir, and Gustave Caillebotte.

One morning as he walked to the atelier, he felt strange. The glow of the green fairy was still with him. Like any hangover, sounds were amplified and the morning sunlight seemed especially bright. Lately, he had been noticing that colors looked more intense, especially the yellows and the greens. He wondered if la fee verte was permanently changing his sensitivity to certain colors.

Upon entering the studio, he found that a large group of students, including Emile and Henri, were gathered around a window and looking at the ballet school in the next building. The men were enjoying the sight of a heavy, full-figured ballet dancer springing across the floor.

"She looks like a wet nurse in a tutu," bellowed Henri as the other young men roared.

"Please refrain from your adolescent interests, gentlemen," ordered Gaston, walking into the room. "Kindly remove yourselves from the window, and be seated at your easels. Today, everyone is going to draw and paint the same study."

As the students listened, Gaston proceeded to introduce an exotic model from North Africa. "This young lady is Mademoiselle Fatima of Algeria. Professeur Cormon will personally inspect everyone's efforts later. His only instruction is that you record the scene exactly as it exists. Do not embellish the setting or change the background. Depict the subject sitting upright. Please remember these instructions."

While removing her robe, the woman ascended the modeling platform. She wore a harem girl's costume with a diaphanous, pink jumper top with long sleeves and bright blue pantaloons. Her olive complexion was emphasized by dark crimson lipstick and metallic makeup about her dark eyes beneath a glittering tiara. She sat at a bench without a backrest.

As the artists prepared their easels and got their materials together for the study at hand, Emile Bernard looked over at van Gogh. "I feel like this is a surprise examination during the inquisition. Do we get the guillotine if we violate the rules?"

Vincent laughed. "Trying to paint a mysterious harem girl without using my creative imagination is next to impossible. Fatima is in for major surgery and a costume change."

"I'm going to do something that should have been done long ago," said Emile, watching the instructor leave the salon. The young fellow got up from his seat and ran into the supply closet in the back of the salon. He came out with cans of paint and two large brushes. In front of the entire class, he walked behind the model and started painting the gray, paint-splattered wall behind the platform with red and green stripes. He worked quickly, and the entire class started laughing, including Fatima.

It did not take Emile very long to paint the background wall. He took the paint and brushes back to the closet and returned to his seat, saying, "Now, that looks a lot better, don't you think?"

"Bravo, my boy, you've scored a victory for anarchists everywhere," said Henri, sitting near the platform in front of the class.

Everyone got back to work, forgetting about Bernard's renovation. The students began the study by first sketching the scene in charcoal and blocking in the tonal qualities with oil paint, starting with the darker tones and moving to the lighter—a standard approach to academic painting for centuries.

Vincent sat in his seat and was unable to sketch the scene. In his mind, it was impossible to translate the scene in terms of foreground, middle ground, and background. He wanted to idealize the scene by searching for its maximum potential. Van Gogh was not afraid to move elements to suit his purpose.

He first portrayed the model lying on a couch rather than sitting on the bench, which encompassed Fatima on three sides. He took away all of her clothing, and she was completely naked with her arms over her head and her legs spread open. Fatima had a dark face, no makeup, and very short hair that stood up on her head. She was frightfully ugly.

He then blocked in the scene, providing tonal values with his oils. He worked from large objects to small details and finished around the same time as everyone else, about 12:30 in the afternoon.

When Professeur Cormon and Gaston came into the room, everyone laughed, remembering Emile's interior decoration. Gaston was the first to notice the striped wall and pointed out the alteration to his superior.

With his hands grasping the lapels of his suit jacket, Cormon bellowed, "What is the meaning of this? Which one of you vandals painted this wall? We cannot have this in my atelier!"

Without meaning to, everyone looked at Emile, who had a guilty look from ear to ear. He stepped forward. "Professeur Cormon, I painted that dirty wall. I think it looks much better."

"You do, Monsieur Bernard? You will wait in my office. Your time here is coming to an end."

Starting at the front of the salon, Cormon made the rounds of the artists' easels. As the professeur examined his students' efforts, he saw that most had followed his instructions and depicted the scene as it actually appeared. His few criticisms pertained to drawing, perspective, or tonal values. Even Emile's canvas copied the scene accurately, including the red and green wall.

Vincent's was the last canvas viewed by the directeur. When his eyes fell upon the bizarre painting, he yelled, "What is this, a caricature by a lunatic?"

"Who are you calling a lunatic?" shouted an enraged van Gogh. "This is what I see in your model. And you have no right to criticize Monsieur Bernard in this manner."

Perplexed, Cormon started to shake like a nervous bird and left the salon. One mutiny in his atelier was all he could handle for one day.

Cormon expelled Emile Bernard from the school. The directeur also wrote a letter addressed to Emile's father stating why he was dismissed.

Later, Emile came back to his seat to get his supplies and spoke to Vincent. "They are throwing me out. Cormon told me to find another atelier."

"You don't need another atelier. We can paint together in the afternoons. We can go to the Louvre, to the top of the butte, or to the northern suburbs. You don't need this school. I'm only here because my room is so small on Rue de Laval."

"Perhaps, I'll go to Brittany. The light and scenery there have always encouraged me."

"No, Emile, let's paint together. Paris has it all. You can go to Brittany next year.

Van Gogh did not realize how close he had become to Emile. He could not bear for his new friend to leave. Previously a loner, Vincent never realized how important a friendship could be.

15

As Vincent experienced the joyous springtime of Paris, many of his insecurities and inhibitions appeared to vanish with the cold. For most of his life, he had seldom spoken with anyone, and his silence had developed into an impediment. But Montmartre was a real training ground, not only for art, but also for life.

In addition to other struggling painters, he was meeting people from all walks of life, each with a story filled with their own dreams and insecurities. This sense of shared destinies gave Vincent the encouragement he needed to expand his world and make new friends.

As Vincent developed his personality, he was still plagued with the deep depression that had drawn him to a solitary existence in the first place. For years, he had been his only friend, instructor, philosopher, and adviser. Like all singular people who spend an inordinate amount of time by themselves, he often held a spirited dialogue with himself. Van Gogh listened to a little voice in his mind that served as a censor or warning device when he tried to fly too high or make a change in his life.

Van Gogh was aware that his imaginary companion had connections to his older brother, who had also been named Vincent Willem, but who died stillborn exactly one year before Vincent was born. He often thought about the small slab of granite that marked his insignificant grave in Brabant, Holland. Van Gogh always felt he was a "replacement child" who really did not belong.

In a moment of depression, when Vincent was having a dialogue with the little voice, he sarcastically called it "Willem." It felt good to disparage this lifelike, cerebral companion by personifying it with a name.

"Shut up, Willem, you son of a bitch! I don't care to deal with your shit, straightaway!"

The anger toward Willem actually worked positively for Vincent. It took away much of the fear and trepidation that often accompanied doing something new or difficult or just requiring courage. But there were times when Willem never spoke a word. The voice was inaudible in the presence of the green fairy of absinthe and when Vincent was making love to a woman, involved in an act of charity, or initially satisfied with a painting.

The rest of the time, Willem was active in van Gogh's mind, especially when van Gogh felt inadequate and inferior to those in the room. Their conversations and confrontations actually gave Willem an opportunity to be heard by someone other than Vincent.

In Cormon's gallery, his classmates and instructors were all potential targets of Willem's wrath. Often, van Gogh would speak rapidly in various languages under his breath as he painted. Some of the younger, high-spirited classmates knew to avoid provoking him. But others were so spirited and mischievous that they could not avoid kidding Vincent. They thought him "cracked but harmless."

One episode that rocked the atelier occurred one quiet morning when Vincent arrived to start another day. As he had always done, he removed his street shoes and went to replace them with the pair of old, paint-encrusted slippers that he wore while working. When he put his feet into the stained footwear, van Gogh could not move because someone had nailed his slippers to the floor. Everyone in attendance burst out into wild laughter. Vincent became enraged, jumped out of the slippers, and ran over to the two students who were laughing the loudest. He grabbed them both around the neck, pushed them down to the floor, and told them to remove the nails from his slippers. The atelier then became very quiet as the two young men sheepishly obeyed the angry artist's request.

Vincent seemed to vary between calm serenity and out-of-control anger and would easily begin arguments with everyone except Henri and Louis Anquetin, whom he respected. When discussing art, very few people could disagree with him.

It was becoming evident to the painters who knew van Gogh best that he would either grow mad or excel beyond any of them. No one contemplated that he might do both.

16

Despite Emile Bernard's dismissal from the atelier, Vincent made sure that he and his closest friend painted together on a regular basis. Having a friend to share in his artistic development dissipated van Gogh's morose mood and stimulated his energy and curiosity. Furthermore, the intellectual atmosphere of Paris, with its modern trends, also challenged the Dutchman, encouraging him to experiment.

On this day, clad in his paint-splattered overalls, van Gogh carried his art materials toward central Paris and the Jardin de Tuileries, the statue-studded gardens designed by Le Notre, the gardener to Louis XVI, who planned the grounds at Versailles.

"Emile, I'm totally captivated by the architecture and parks of this City of Lights. They seem to stimulate my creativity and vision."

"Yes, but it seems that half of Paris has found the Tuileries on this warm day."

As birds chirped among the blooming daffodils and red tulips, the artists found a vantage point to set up their easels. Fountains shot their water into the sky as mothers with baby carriages walked on the same grounds where a royal palace once stood. Only the tranquil gardens remain.

When Emile unpacked his painting supplies, he brought out a copy of the popular magazine, *Paris Illustre*. On its cover was *The Courtesan,* a Japanese woodblock print by Keisai Eisen from the 1820's.

Seeing the magazine, van Gogh commented, "Everywhere you look today, you see the Japanese style. It's like an invasion from the Far East."

"Yes, Gogh, Japanese style, design, and all manner of art has burst upon the scene like a bombshell. They say *Japonisme* is as important to modern art as classical antiquity had been for the Renaissance."

"Yes, I am starting to notice that the other students at Cormon's have been incorporating Japanese influences into their paintings. Henri and Louis are expert in the Japanese style of heavy contours, bounded areas of pure color, and flat compositions."

"Unfortunately," said Emile, "Professeur Cormon has no interest in the Japanese influence."

Van Gogh was first fascinated with Japanese prints when he studied in Antwerp, but today he decided to experiment with their application of pure color as a powerful conduit of emotion. He knew that his painting was starving from a lack of bold, daring color.

As he painted the Parisians strolling through the colorful gardens, he explored pastel tones—soft blues, yellows, and pinks—colors that reflected the air and energy of Paris.

During the rest of the spring and summer, van Gogh continued to experiment with all things Japanese. He read everything he could about the Far East and became infatuated by Japanese culture, particularly the dignity and beauty of Asian women. He hoped that someday he could travel to Japon and capture its lovely scenes and qualities of its people in his painting. At the same time, his palette that had been so dark during his earlier period was becoming lighter and more colorful.

17

While walking through Place Pigalle, Vincent had to stop several times to wait for Henri as he hobbled along on his short legs and cherrywood cane. The Dutch immigrant was becoming a Parisian and was by now a boulevardier, a frequenter of the cafés on the boulevard. He went not only to drink but to read the gazette and talk to his peers and friends. The café was his family, especially since he was unmarried.

Within recent years, there had been changes in the cafés. Le Chat Noir opened on Boulevard Rouchechouart and provided customers with entertainment. Artist Rudolphe Salis gave up his paintbrush for a piano and started one of the first café-concerts, even though it was illegal to play a musical instrument inside a café. At first, little shows at Le Chat Noir consisted of songs and jokes focused on ordinary events of life, love, and politics, but eventually the bustling nightclub presented all types of singers, dancers, comedians, and light shows. Some of the café-concerts gradually turned into large music halls, such as the Follies-Bergére.

Most café-concerts possessed a complete lack of formality. Audiences came and went at whatever point in the night's entertainment they pleased. Almost any attire was acceptable, and food and drink were served throughout the performances.

Furthermore, no longer did a Frenchman just go to the café to drink wine. Now, he drank beer or liqueur such as absinthe, vermouth, or bitters. This seemed to be the fashion ever since the World Exhibition of 1867, when German, Italian, and English barmaids were first seen in Paris.

Waitresses took the place of waiters in many of the new beer saloons in Paris and Montmartre. Owners of the bistros got the idea to costume the waitresses in charming outfits that depicted foreign or exotic locations.

Tonight, the men were visiting Café de la Nouvelle-Athenes, a gathering spot for Montmartre's leading writers and artists, decorated in the Grecian style. Henri had told Vincent that this café was frequented by Emile Zola, their favorite contemporary novelist.

The café was full of customers this warm evening, and the artists looked for an empty table or a recognizable face among the chatty patrons. Suddenly, some chairs in the back of the room became free, and Henri and Vincent made a dash to the table.

Standing in the middle of the little stage in the front of the café was a strange-looking man in a large black hat. He also wore a red shirt, black velvet cape, high boots, and a red scarf. "That's Aristide Bruant, the *chanteur*," remarked Henri. "He's made a living attacking the comfortable and lamenting the struggles of the poor."

Bruant was in the middle of an abusive but entertaining confrontation with a well-dressed couple sitting at a table near the stage. "You call your lady friend an example of the upper classes? Monsieur, my poodle has better features."

"Oh, really?" responded the customer. "Well, you are the worst singer I've ever heard."

"That may be, my good fellow, but tomorrow my voice might improve, and your woman will still look like a dog."

The crowd went wild and yelled for Bruant to sing one of his *chansons*. Stroking his guitar, the tall, long-faced Bruant lamented:

> *They are those with no more charm*
> *Not a penny in their hose.*
> *Street-walkers, Sidewalk-stompers,*
>
> *They walk at night, when there's no more light,*
> *On the sidewalks, hair frizz, breasts ablaze, feet worn away.*
>
> *Christ with mild eyes, who died for our lives,*
> *Warm the earth where holes are dug for them.*

The audience clapped its approval, and Bruant took a slow bow, stating he would return later in the evening.

Looking around the café, which was decorated in a classical Mediterranean style, Henri asked, "Gogh, do you see anyone we know?"

"You're asking me, Latrec? You're the one with the string of associates."

A waitress dressed in a Grecian toga presented herself, and the men both ordered absinthe with a side glass of brandy. It was a potent combination that Henri termed "the earthquake."

As Vincent, looked around the café, he noticed a dark-haired, attractive woman sitting with some dignified gentlemen in the corner of the room. She was one of the only women in the café and looked out of place in the presence of so many male customers. Actually, it was rare for women to frequent these cafés, especially alone. However, to be escorted by gentlemen was quite acceptable.

"Who is that young woman sitting at the corner table?"

"Oh, that, my friend, is Suzanne Valadon, a very interesting model who is also learning to paint. She has come a long way from a miserable beginning. Suzanne's a single mother raising a son."

"Whom is she sitting with? They look like two lawyers."

"Well, you are correct about one of them. Artist Edward Degas doesn't work as a lawyer anymore. He's the man with the dark complexion."

"Oh yes, I've seen his work in Theo's shop," said van Gogh.

"The other man with the glasses is no less than Emile Zola, the writer."

"Zola! You said he might be here. Henri, I've read many of his books. The man is a genius."

"Keep your voice down, Gogh. If he sees you looking at him, he'll run for the Champs-Elysees. I know both Suzanne and Edward. They'll introduce us to Zola. But you cannot act anxious, and refrain from peppering him with questions about his writings."

Zola was considered one of France's most perceptive and erudite personalities. His opinion of art, politics, and sociology was widely followed by the intelligentsia of Paris and beyond. Vincent had read several of his novels about the fictitious Rougon-Marquart family. In the series, Zola utilized his "naturalistic method" to study the effects of heredity and environment on the members of a single family. The writer held that life is predestined, and a person cannot overcome his background. Zola's most popular novel in the saga, *Nana*, shocked polite French society when it was published in 1880. It sold fifty-five thousand copies in its first day. The racy story of a shameless courtesan during the Second Empire of Louis-Philippe, Napoleon's nephew, outraged the conservative and religious elements of Parisian society.

"Henri, should we just walk over and say hello to Suzanne?"

"No, she'll come over when she sees me. She's been posing for me twice a week."

"Do you sleep with her?"

"Why of course, at least once a week. She's a very amiable young woman who I am becoming very fond of." Despite her hard life, she has a wonderful, alluring face. Degas has painted her many times and is also currently working with her."

"Does Degas also sleep with her?"

"Some say he does. But I think Degas is a dried-up old lawyer who doesn't have sex with anyone. He's another who claims it saps his strength for the creative process. It has been said that his platonic affair with an American female artist, Mary Cassat, has actually become an *affaire d'amour*, but I do not believe it."

"Latrec, keep quiet! Here comes Suzanne. She has recognized you."

With a smile on her face, Suzanne Valadon approached the men's table.

"How are you, Henri?"

"Ah, Suzanne, you are looking very well this evening. Let me introduce another painter from Atelier Cormon, Vincent van Gogh."

"*Chantee-me*, mademoiselle," bowed van Gogh. "Is that Emile Zola at your table? What is he doing here?"

"Well, it is propitious you two are here. Monsieur Zola is organizing a protest among artists and writers against the proposed tower of Gustave Eiffel."

Suzanne took the two men back to her table, and after the introductions, they were seated next to Zola.

"Gentlemen," said the author, "I'm spearheading a petition among the creative artisans of Paris to protest the building of this monstrous structure."

Degas interrupted. "Oui, it will be the tallest structure in the world, over three hundred meters high."

Zola continued. "Oui, we must protest the tower with all our vigor and indignation, in the name of good taste. French art and history are endangered."

"Monsieur Zola," Vincent added, "I am formally of the Netherlands, but as an artist I appreciate the elegance and proportion of Paris. This tower sounds like a blemish on the face of our fair city."

"Oui, monsieur, the way I understand it, the structure will consist of two distinct parts, a base composed of a platform resting on four supports. And as these supports taper upward, a slender tower will rise above a second platform."

"That sounds hideous. Where is this tower going to be built?" asked Henri.

"On the parade grounds of the Ecole Militaire, near the river Seine. It will act as the center to the World's Fair of 1889," answered Zola.

"Oh, thank God, it's only temporary. We could not endure such a permanent disgrace in our city," said Degas.

"Well, my mission is to stop the construction, which right now is scheduled to begin January next. Charles Garnier, the marvelous architect of the Opera House, has signed our petition, and I hope you two artists would also give your signatures."

"We would be most pleased," said Henri. "Where will the petition be presented, Monsieur Zola?"

"We will present the petition to the municipal government at Hotel de Ville next week."

After signing the petition, Vincent remembered he was in the presence of his favorite writer. "Monsieur Zola, may I ask you something?"

Henri closed his eyes.

"What is that, Monsieur van Gogh?"

"In *Nana*, you write about the analogy between religious and sexual fervor. Can one exist in the presence of the other?"

"Ah, well, that's a discussion for another night."

"No, monsieur, I would like to hear your answer."

Van Gogh did not care that the other people sitting at the table were made uncomfortable by his insistence.

"To answer your query, religion is a complex element of our society," responded Zola. "It provides the meaning and motivation for many, which allows life to proceed in the face of contingencies and great changes."

"But monsieur," interjected Vincent, "despite all his technological advances, man, in strategic respects, remains powerless in the conflict between his own needs and the limitations of his environment."

"Oui, but religion's function is to provide meaning and motivation in the face of powerlessness, frustration, and deprivation. And please forgive me, mademoiselle ... I believe there is nothing apart from a woman's vagina and religion. They both propel a man into sustained action. Sometimes they coexist. Look at all the churches in Montmartre, the hub of our sexual world."

Laughter broke the tense atmosphere. Even Vincent, who had many more questions, laughed. "Thank you Monsieur. I'm very fond of your books."

"Well, Monsieur van Gogh, I hope, someday, to see your paintings. For now, I must be on my way. It was a pleasure speaking with everyone, and thanks for signing my petition."

With that, Zola quickly left the table and walked out of the café. The people at the table sat in silence before Henri spoke. "Well, Vincent, you certainly know how to start and end a conversation."

"Obviously, he's a man of very well-chosen words," said Degas. "I hope you were not offended, Suzanne."

"No, but let's change the subject. Henri, do you think Professeur Cormon is ready to admit women to his atelier? Many of the academics are starting additional classes for only women, alongside normal instruction."

"I cannot say, Suzanne. Cormon is having a troublesome time presently with his male students. His lack of discipline and structure is encouraging a few mutinies among the students lately."

"Why would such an attractive woman want to become an artist?" asked Vincent. "You should marry while you're still young."

"You men have it easy. If you marry, you acquire a housekeeper, a model, and a brush washer. When a female artist marries, she perishes as an artist."

"Accept my apology, mademoiselle," said Vincent in a friendly tone. "I only say it is *difficile* for most artists to earn a living these days."

With that explanation, van Gogh bade farewell to Degas and Suzanne. He then turned and left the table with Lautrec not far behind.

18

Walking like three men on an important mission, Theo, Vincent, and Emile hurried down Rue Laffitte. On this sunny afternoon, they were attending the Eighth Impressionist's Exhibition.

"This could be the last of these shows," said Theo, walking in the middle. "I understand the organizers had difficulty convincing the original Impressionists to exhibit."

"Monet has gotten so successful, he probably feels he does not need the others anymore," offered Bernard. "I just hope my friend Paul Gauguin did not leave for Pont-Aven straightaway."

"Is he not the Peruvian artist that others call 'a wolf without a leash'?" asked Theo.

"The same, but he's a talented artist who knows how to use color. He's been working with colorizing ceramics before they are fired in the oven. We painted in Brittany together, before I entered Cormon's."

Arriving at the Maison Doree restaurant, adjacent to Boulevard des Italiens, Theo handed the attendant in the foyer three admission tickets. The men climbed to the second floor, where the seventeen exhibiting artists had rented five large rooms. The catalogue listed 246 items. Upon entering the exhibition, Vincent noticed that many attendees had formed a queue outside the last salon on the floor.

"They are here to see the painting by George Seurat," said Theo. "It's causing quite a stir."

"I'm too impatient to wait in a queue," said Vincent. "Let's go through the whole exhibit, and we'll look at Seurat before we leave." Though curious about Seurat, the others agreed and began by viewing the other segments of the show.

Vincent was excited to see these paintings and their creators in the same proximity. The American Impressionist Mary Cassat stood next to her works *Woman Sewing in the Garden* and *Child in a Straw Hat*. Vincent was very interested in her technique. Her use of warm colors and soft lighting captured his attention.

"Mademoiselle, you bring out the emotions of your subjects in your paintings."

"Yes, monsieur, I try my best. That's all we can do in life."

Van Gogh thought her French was excellent, but she seemed quite distant and reserved. She continued to answer van Gogh's questions with polite but generally vague answers.

After strolling into the next room, Vincent could not easily view the series of pastel works of Edgar Degas. Many people crowded around the paintings. Degas, himself, was huddled in one corner, answering the questions of a newspaper art critic.

"Monsieur Degas looks and sounds like a lawyer who's defending himself in court," remarked Emile.

Entitled collectively *Series of Female Nudes, Bathing, Washing, Drying, Cleansing, Combing Their Hair or Having It Combed,* the exhibit of ten paintings showed women in their toilette tending to their bodies.

"Ah, this is a novel but racy theme," noted Theo. "It looks as if the women are unaware they're being watched."

"Oui," added Emile, "it gives one the impression of a voyeur peering through a keyhole into the privacy of a cocotte's sanctuary."

"I disagree with you both," replied Vincent. "These works might depict an unconventional scene, but they are not at all degrading."

To avoid the endless questions from his newspaper inquisitors, Degas walked over to the three men. "Ah, messieurs, I see you have found my new work."

Van Gogh was the first to react. "Edgar, I think your treatment is marvelous. Screw the art critics, if they cannot grasp the honesty and frankness of your pastels."

"Merci, Vincent, I appreciate your support. And bravo to you, my boy. The manner in which you debated Zola on the philosophy of religion the other night was quite impressive." Degas then turned to Vincent's brother. "Theo, I have already sold half of these paintings, and the exhibition is not yet over."

Van Gogh was both exhilarated and depressed. He liked to hear about artists who were successful in selling their work. But it also reminded him that he had never known the joy of selling one of his own paintings.

Theo was very encouraged by Degas's success and scheduled a meeting for the following week about the possibility of selling his remaining paintings at Boussod & Valadon.

In the next salon, a large, red-faced artist in a blue sailor's shirt stood near his paintings. His steadfast frown was lifted into a broad smile when he recognized Emile Bernard coming into view.

"Emile, it is good to see you, my young friend. Thanks for coming."

"Oh, I would not miss this exhibition. I'm just glad you hadn't left for Brittany and Pont-Aven."

"I don't know, maybe next month. But who are your associates?"

"Paul Gauguin, these are my friends, Messieurs Vincent and Theo van Gogh."

While firmly shaking their hands, Gauguin added, "Oui, I've heard of these gentlemen. Theo, you're the manager of Boussod's Gallery. And Vincent, you are manager of Professeur Cormon."

"I see word gets around," said Vincent. "Someone has to restrain Cormon, now that Emile is on his own."

"I'm glad Emile is out of Cormon's. I've been trying to convince him to come paint in Pont-Aven with me."

Emile did not react but changed the subject. "Paul, show us the paintings you have on display."

"These are my most recent, *The Beach at Dieppe* and *A Still Life of Fruit with Charles Laval's Profile.*"

"Why of course, that's Charles, the art student," said Vincent. "I see him every day at Cormon's. I must say, I am intrigued by your colors. They add a subjective and unique element to your work."

"It's my mother's Inca blood. I see what I feel. Reality only exists as I perceive and express it."

Van Gogh quickly added, "And your colors change the mood and put your own stamp on the painting."

"I like you, Vincent. Maybe you and Emile should come paint with me. We'll go to Asniers and the northern suburbs sometime."

"That would be excellent, Paul. I look forward to that."

Theo interrupted by saying, "Speaking of Asniers, is that not near the scene of Monsieur Seurat's painting, the one in the next room … our next stop?"

"Go see for yourselves. It's amazing. It took Seurat two years of constant work to complete the painting," said Gauguin. "Go, quickly."

After bidding adieu, the men set off to the last room of the exhibition. Fortunately, there was no one in line. As they entered, they were almost overwhelmed by one enormous painting. *A Sunday Afternoon on the Island of La Grande Jatte* measured more than ten feet across. But it was not the painting's size that mesmerized the men; it was the technique of the artist. The images in the painting were comprised of tiny dots of pure color. A border of these tiny dots added a colorful frame to the giant masterpiece.

Van Gogh stayed for over an hour studying the painting. He was intrigued by the way Seurat had carefully placed dots of pure color in relationship to one another so that when the picture was viewed from a distance, the dots seemed to blend to form a new color. He discerned that this *mélange optique* produced more lively color effects than if the paints had been physically mixed together. Van Gogh was disappointed that the artist was not in attendance. As he turned to leave, Vincent noted, "This, my friends, is a revolution in the world of art."

What van Gogh and his colleagues had witnessed was the birth of Neo-Impressionism. The term was coined by art-critic Felix Feneon when he viewed Seurat's painting at the eighth and last Impressionist Exhibition. Seurat's technique of applying precise dots of paint would become known as pointillism.

19

One warm spring evening while van Gogh was exploring Montmartre, he encountered a gauntlet of more than twenty prostitutes along the sidewalk on Rue Fontaine. Most were quite young, aged between fifteen and twenty. These *filles de joie* were talkative and brushed up against the strolling artist, telling him in very descriptive French what they were willing to do. The youngest girls looked uncomfortable and out of place in their wobbly high-heeled shoes and stiff corsets.

"Where do you rush off, monsieur?" cried one of the older girls. "Let's go somewhere so I can show you what I've got!"

"No, mademoiselle, I'm a poor art student who is late for an important appointment. Please, let me pass."

"Oh ya, you an art student. You're old enough to be my father."

The comment created a whimsical silence in which Vincent made eye contact with the woman. Lucette was about twenty-five and quite appealing to the Dutchman. She read his mind and followed Vincent down the street, convinced she had a potential customer.

"If you're an art student, maybe you're looking for an experienced model," continued Lucette. "Pay four francs for my pussy, and the modeling is free. Isn't that a satisfactory offer?"

"I'm a starving artist, and all I can afford is two francs."

Realizing she had gotten the price she intended, Lucette agreed. "Okay, but I must get back here on Rue du Faubourg in an hour."

Within fifteen minutes, Lucette was naked before van Gogh in his room. He was intrigued by her raven black hair, alabaster skin, and shapely body. But before he made love to her, he wanted to create a permanent record. Vincent had her sit in a chair and did a pencil sketch of her in the faint light of his room. Shadows emphasized her bare shoulders and the curvature of her throat, collarbone, and breasts. Her hair tumbled loosely, and her sparkling blue eyes looked at the artist in a submissive and suggestive gaze.

As he drew, he asked Lucette about herself. She was very talkative and told of coming to Paris at sixteen from the town of Cassis on the *Côte d'Azur* near

Marseille. She was hired as a countergirl at Galleries Lafayette, a department store along the grand boulevards near the Opera.

Later, she was selected to be a mannequin and would stroll around the store showing off the latest in couture fashion. Lucette then met a man who convinced her to quit her job and become an artists' model. He was actually a *maquereau*, or pimp, who got her modeling assignments where she also had to sleep with the artist.

Lucette went on to tell van Gogh that, within a few months, she had become pregnant. When she refused to risk an abortion in a farmhouse on the top of La Buttes, her man abandoned her.

As Vincent drew the woman's portrait and heard her story, his compassionate nature appeared to take over the scene. His desire seemed to drain out of his body like air rushing from a balloon. He finished the drawing in about thirty minutes.

"You can put your clothes back on, my dear."

"What about the rest?" asked Lucette. "You're a strange one, monsieur."

"Some say I'm an eccentric, a disagreeable man. But I want my work to show what is in the heart of such an eccentric, of such a nobody."

"I hope you will find what you are seeking, monsieur."

"Merci, Lucette. I believe we are quite finished here."

Van Gogh gave the woman four francs and sent her on her way.

20

As summer settled upon Paris, Vincent and Theo found that their small flat was no longer suitable. The artists' canvases, paints, and supplies had overrun the room. When Theo returned in the evening, he was faced with piles of dirty dishes and paint-stained clothing.

Furthermore, Vincent would not let him sleep, as he wanted to talk about art and the art market far into the night. Vincent was also tiring of Cormon's atelier now that his friend Emile Bernard had been banned from the studio.

The brothers decided to move to a larger apartment at fifty-four Rue Lepic, halfway up the west side of the butte. Two large wooden doors off the sidewalk shielded the entrance from the street. Beyond the doors was a small courtyard with a turnaround for a horse and carriage.

The flat was spacious with two separate bedrooms and a living room. In addition, Vincent got his own studio with plenty of light provided by a southern exposure.

The artist was elated by the move to the new flat and tossed and turned all night in anticipation of waking up in his new surroundings. As the subtle, pre-dawn light invaded the darkness, Vincent rose from his bed and slipped on a pair of trousers, together with an old woolen sweater. Like a sleepwalker, he trudged out the door of the flat and down the hallway of the building on Rue Lepic. At the end of the hall, he climbed the stairs that led to the roof.

Upon opening the door, he was overwhelmed by the sky's pink hue. The distant sun was slowly rising behind the black silhouettes of neighboring buildings. Before the Dutchman lay a panoramic view of Paris. Only a few structures obscured his view of the southern horizon. Below, he could hear the thud of the street cleaners' wooden clogs as they swept the quiet sidewalks with their brooms. From the scene, Vincent drew a calm serenity that engendered a feeling of contentment and well-being.

"What are you doing up here?" said Theo as he sat down next to his brother on the roof. "When you failed to return to the flat, I came looking for you."

"Theo, you were right. Montmartre and the city of Paris are marvelous. Even though the air is chilly this morning, there's a life to it. It must be the energy of the people, all with different dreams for themselves." A cabriolet clattered down the street. "Even that Parisian cab horse looks like he cannot wait to get to his next destination," remarked Vincent.

"Yes, but doesn't he know that it's a journey that never ends for him until he's dead?"

"But Theo, that's life for all of us. I often feel that I am part of a great chain of artists that came before and will come after me. We strive for some new idea that makes our imaginations a reality. After I pass on, another person with a roomful of paints and canvases will try his hand at it."

"But Cent, it all adds up to something. Look at all the centuries of art in all the museums and galleries throughout the world."

"Because of you, I am a part of the art world. It's like a dream come true. I owe you so much."

"You owe me nothing. When we sell your paintings, then we will decide what you owe me as your agent."

"I don't know when I am going to sell my paintings, and every month you give me a hundred-fifty francs. So, from now on, I want you to have possession of all my work."

"No, Cent, you don't have to do that."

"No, it's all I can give you in payment. After all, you have given me a new life. You have introduced me to some of France's best artists and taken me to the best exhibitions. I no longer feel like a hermit, an outcast, or a strange eccentric whom everyone ignores."

"Indeed, you have made close friends among some great artists. Many search you out to get your views and thoughts on various topics."

"Yes, I've been socializing well with those at the atelier and at night in the cafés, but I fear my melancholy has returned with its sadness and hopelessness."

"The way you felt last year at home in Nuenen?"

"Oui, but somehow it's worse now. I am easily irritated and lose control in front of the other artists. One moment, I'm content with my life. In the next, I'm overwhelmingly depressed and anxious."

"Are there certain times of the day that are worse than others?"

"Well, when I'm immersed in my work during the day, I'm usually in control. But as day passes into early evening, I start to feel badly again. In the night, the emotional pain is only relieved by drinking. Of course, the sex of a woman is another soothing diversion."

"Do you sleep well at night?

"As long as I am drunk, I have no trouble going to sleep. But I awaken many times during the night with dreams, dark and foreboding."

"Vincent, you may be drinking too much absinthe. They say it is a very powerful substance that can injure your health."

"Unfortunately, I feel that without the green fairy, I would totally fall apart."

"Cent, maybe you should not dwell on your own anxieties but think about positive things, like finding a good woman in Paris."

"I wouldn't mind hooking up with that old girlfriend of yours, Agostina. But I can't find the nerve to approach her."

"Oh, Cent, she's a little crazy. I admit that for an older woman she's quite alluring, but she's been through a lot. Before I met her, she had been the companion of artist Edouard Dantan. Their affair lasted more than ten years. They separated before she started the café. She apparently was a very successful model and accumulated enough savings to open the café. Some say, she was also aided by an inheritance from the Barbizon artist Jean-Baptiste Corot."

"She seems quite pleasant, even though she's in a tough business."

"Yes, she can also be quite demanding with a fiery temper."

"But Theo, anything's better than the hopeless whores that I usually end up with. They would sell themselves for two francs to anyone."

21

Once he became acclimated to the new neighborhood, van Gogh liked to roam around and set up his portable easel when he found a scene that sparked his interest. He particularly liked painting well-composed scenes in outdoor cafés and the view of the city of Paris from the top walkways of Montmartre.

About six weeks after the brothers had moved into their new apartment, Vincent was walking through Place Pigalle after a full day at the atelier. He was very fond of strolling the streets of Montmartre in the evenings, even though he had been told it could be dangerous. Many of his fellow artists walked with a sturdy cane for protection, and some carried pistols. This Dutchman felt splendid in his new gentleman's wardrobe, purchased by Theo at a local haberdasher.

The artist was starting to enjoy dressing up, mainly because he desired to fit in with the other artists at the atelier. Most were young bon vivant who looked quite dashing in their frock coats, ties, and three-piece suits. Moreover, Vincent appeared more affluent than the aggregate of his personal wealth, which still fit inside a cardboard box. He usually carried only a few francs in his pocket.

In Place Pigalle, cabarets, cheap dance halls, and bars lined the intersection. People walking at either a quick or a slow pace crammed the sidewalks. The fast pedestrians had a destination, while the loiterers were selling something. Women in bright dresses asked men if they wanted to have a good time. Men offered cocottes of quality, opium, or stolen goods. There were also barkers outside the various bars along the street, coaxing gentlemen to come inside.

As Vincent walked down the street, he noticed a tall, strapping man with blue eyes and blond hair looking at him intently. In Dutch, the man asked, "*Bent u van Amsterdam?*"

Vincent answered, "*Nee, ik van Nughen.* No, I am from Nuenen."

"Well, I am Willem. Finally, I meet another Dutchman! What is your name, monsieur?"

"My name is Vincent."

"Ah, Vincent, do you want to see the sexiest show in all of Paris? It shan't cost you anything."

At that point, the artist had a feeling it had been a mistake to speak to this fellow countryman.

"Monsieur, we are both Dutchmen. I wouldn't steer you wrong. What can you lose? The first drink is without charge, and you see a great show, very sexy girls."

Before Vincent could respond, the big Dutchman escorted him through the door of the La Caverne. Once past the front door, he saw a steep flight of stairs appearing to descend into hell's underworld. Van Gogh got a strange feeling in his stomach as he walked down the stairs. He was not certain if it was fear or just the anticipation of seeing the sexiest show in Paris.

At the bottom of the steps were swinging doors with little glass windows. He pushed the doors open and walked into the very dark space. The only light was provided by a gaslight on the wall above a little stage. Painted a dull, flat purple, the walls and the stage were empty, except for a naked, wooden chair.

As he tried to orient himself, the soothing voice of a woman greeted van Gogh. "Bonsoir, monsieur, you've come for the show. I am Estelle. Please walk this way."

Estelle sat Vincent at a small table against the wall. Walking away, she added, "The show will start shortly, monsieur."

Vincent felt alone in the dark as his eyes became accustomed to the dim light of La Caverne. He heard hushed voices to his right. There sat another gentleman speaking with a young woman. That table was also against the wall but closer to the swinging doors. The artist had to look over his right shoulder to see both the couple and the stage with its chair at the far end of the room.

Directly across from Vincent's table, a small bar encircled a short, muscular man. With arms folded across his chest, the bartender stared at Vincent with black eyes that had no trouble piercing the darkness.

A large, buxom woman in a white blouse and black dress appeared next to the table. "Bonsoir! My name is Marie. May I sit with you as we watch the show?"

Without waiting for an answer, Marie sat down with Vincent. Estelle instantly reappeared. "Monsieur, what would you like for your free drink?"

"You may bring me an absinthe, *raide*—straight, Estelle."

"Ah, raide, a real Parisian. You don't find them so easily anymore." She looked at Marie. "And what can I get for you, Mademoiselle Marie?"

"I would like the same, la fee verte, please, madame."

As Estelle went over to the bar to get the drinks, Marie lit a candle in the middle of the table. The light cast a yellow glow on her throat and chest. Her blouse was opened to the waist, revealing her décolletage with its cleavage.

"So tell me, monsieur, do you live in Montmartre, or are you just a visitor?"

"I live here now. I'm a painter from *la Hollande*."

Estelle returned with the drinks and placed them on the table. The small glasses of green absinthe shone like emeralds through the candlelight.

Marie picked up her glass, "Oh, la Hollande. Willem, who works out front, is from Amsterdam. But he's no artist, I can assure you, *mon ami*."

Vincent was becoming bored by the conversation and asked, "When will the show begin. What's it like?"

"Oh, the show? Juliana is a very seductive woman, but she is late again this evening. The bartender, Louis, is very upset with her again."

Like a shadow, Estelle appeared at Vincent's table again. "May I get you two lovebirds another drink?"

Vincent was starting to smell a rat that was getting bigger by the minute. He said loudly, "When does this damn show start? I ... we don't want any more drinks."

Estelle answered, "Please calm down. You'll upset the other customers. Besides, Juliana is here. She's just arrived. Have one more drink. The show will begin, and you'll be glad you waited."

Marie left her chair and came over and sat down next to Vincent against the wall. She pressed the side of her breast against his arm and placed his hand on the top of her thigh.

At about the same time, Estelle presented the bill to the gentleman at the nearby table. There was a loud outburst, and the man jumped up, shouting, "What! Are you people crazy? Sixty francs for two drinks? I won't pay it."

With those words, the choreography began. Louis, the bartender, leaped over the bar with a heavy club and ran to the swinging doors. Willem, the big Dutchman, suddenly appeared and stood shoulder to shoulder with the club-wielding bartender. They both stared menacingly at the gentleman, who fell into his chair as if he was about to lose consciousness.

Estelle got back to business. "Well, monsieur, what about *l'addition*? The check, it's sixty francs."

"It takes a railway man a month to earn sixty francs. I just don't carry that much money with me."

The young woman, who previously was amusing the gentleman, added her contribution. "What do you think, monsieur, you can go to a show with a respectable woman, drinking and laughing, and not expect to pay for it?"

The man looked over at the bartender, who by now was slapping the palm of his hand with the club. The gentleman stood up, brought out his wallet, and emptied his pockets. "You see, all I have is forty-two francs. You can have it. It's all I have."

Estelle became very understanding. "All right, monsieur, if that's all you have. We will accept it, but of course you'll throw in that pocket watch."

The man was going to start arguing again but stopped himself. He threw down his watch and picked up his coat. Willem opened the door for the man, who ran up the stairs to his freedom. The big Dutchman then closed the door and calmly looked over at Vincent. The bartender put the club back under the bar.

The artist watched the drama unfold and realized he had just witnessed the only kind of show that ever took place at La Caverne. Juliana was a permanent no-show. Vincent's mind went blank, and he needed time to think about what he should do. Most people would be fearful in this situation, but not Vincent van Gogh.

Vincent stood up and asked to be shown the water closet. He walked into the restroom, which was just a bare hole in the broken tile floor. There was no way to get out, no window. La Caverne was below ground for a reason.

Vincent came out of the water closet and put his pipe in his mouth. He went directly to the bar and asked the bartender for a match to light his pipe. Louis responded with an ugly grin that showed his rotted teeth through black stubble.

As the bartender fumbled for a match, Vincent scoured the bar with his eyes. He could not locate the club. Louis found the match and held it out to the artist with his right hand. His other arm was under the counter of the bar.

Vincent struck the match, but instead of lighting his pipe, he pushed the flame into Louis's face. The bartender stepped back and drew the club from under the bar. The two men grabbed onto the club with both hands. The bartender had the handle and pulled it with all of his brute strength toward his own face.

Rather than trying to wrestle the club from Louis's strong grip, Vincent used the man's strength to jam the handle right into the mouth of the bartender. The end of the club broke the man's front teeth and slid to the back of his throat. Louis threw his hands to his mouth, and blood gushed through his fingers.

After drawing the club from the man's face, Vincent ran toward the door, but Willem blocked his escape. As the burly man put his arms up to reach for the club, Vincent swung it toward the man's legs. A horrible cracking sound was heard as it made contact with his left knee. Crying in pain, Willem crashed to the floor like a felled oak tree. Vincent was prepared to hit him again, but Marie covered the huge Dutchman's body with her own, begging van Gogh to leave.

22

The agitated painter peeked over his shoulder more than once as he walked hurriedly from Place Pigalle. He was sure no one was in pursuit, but his hands were still shaking from the incident in La Caverne.

Approaching the flat on Rue Lepic, he remembered that his brother was away on business, traveling south to Marseille. Theo would not be home until the following evening.

Deciding it was crucial to behold a friendly face, the artist thought about Agostina and Café du Tambourin. He turned around and headed down the hill toward the boulevard.

When Vincent arrived at the cabaret, the dining tables were empty, as it was too early for dinner. A waitress was setting up one of the tables, while two waiters, muttering about the dishonesty of horse racing, sat in chairs along the wall.

The bar, however, had a few patrons. Vincent gained the attention of the bartender. "An absinthe, raide, with a cube of sugar, *s'il vous plaît.*"

Alongside the bar stood the usual shady characters, but in light of the evening's previous events, they did not look very menacing to van Gogh. Picking up his drink, the artist turned and asked very boldly, "How are you fine gentlemen getting along this evening?"

The thugs drew blank expressions, shrugged their shoulders, and turned away.

"And how are you getting along tonight, Vincent? Where are your friends?"

He turned back to the bar, and there stood Agostina near the bartender. She had just arrived at the café and looked bright and cheerful with freshly applied makeup. She wore a pink silk dress with amber trim, and her dark hair was set with a single, wide braid that flowed down her back.

"I am alone tonight, Agostina. I guess everyone else is busy."

"So, you thought of my place. Should I be flattered, or is it just the food?"

"I believe I just wanted to see a friendly face."

"Oh, is that your reason for talking with these losers at the bar?" she said laughing. "Come in the back, and I'll fix a table. You look like you need an early dinner."

Vincent sat by himself at a table by the kitchen as Agostina personally served him. She brought out some wine and a meal of *stracotto al Barolo*, beef braised in wine. She sat with him as he ate the beef drenched in thick, tasty sauce, together with French bread.

"So, you did come for the food, after all."

"No, I came for the pleasure of looking at you. You are the most splendid woman on this boulevard." Agostina was an emotional woman, and Vincent was not sure if she was going to laugh or cry over his flattering words.

It was not everyday that a man spoke so kindly in her establishment. "Why are you alone tonight?" she asked.

"I don't know. I didn't make any plans. Theo is away on a business trip to Marseille. I'm all alone in that giant flat."

"Oh yes, that giant flat, where you have to go out in the hall to turn around."

"Oh no, we have just moved into a much larger flat on Rue Lepic, a few blocks from here."

"Do you have your own studio?"

"Yes, I do. But my paintings and artist's supplies seem to spread themselves all over the flat. Tina, would you like to see my paintings?"

Suddenly, the room got very noisy as the tables started to fill up with hungry customers. In a quiet voice, the former model said, "Oh, Vincent, after all I have been through with your brother, I do not care to start something with you."

"Please, Agostina, I just want to spend a little time with you away from the restaurant. My life is tied up in my paintings. You were an artist's model. Surely you know how important they are to me."

Agostina stood up from the table, and Vincent's heart sank into his full stomach. She looked down at the floor, avoiding the artist's eyes. "I really shouldn't," she said, looking away at the other tables. "Maybe, if things aren't busy tonight. Could you come back at eleven, and we will see?"

Later that night, Vincent escorted Agostina down the quiet boulevard and through the side streets toward his flat. They were both nervous, but that made the rendezvous that much more exciting, as both held an emptiness in their lives.

Once inside the flat, Vincent prepared a heavily diluted and sweetened absinthe for each of them. As she sipped her milky liqueur, Agostina sat on the couch in the flat's living room.

"Did you paint all the paintings in this room?"

"Yes, on this wall is my latest study. It depicts people strolling along a shady lane at Luxembourg Garden last Sunday."

"You have captured a very tranquil scene of people enjoying their afternoon."

Moving down the wall, Vincent continued his museum-type tour by describing several more landscapes he had painted around Montmartre and central Paris.

Agostina interrupted him when she noticed a painting of a worn, old pair of shoes on another wall. "Is that also yours? It looks like it was painted by a different artist during a different time."

"Yes, that is also mine." Van Gogh thought she probably did not like the monochrome tones and limited color in the painting, which generated an old-world look. Vincent had completed the painting when he had first come to Montmartre in March.

Agostina broke the silence. "That's an interesting portrait in the corner."

"Oh, that's my first self-portrait, recently completed."

The painting illustrated Vincent's frame of mind and change in appearance since arriving in Paris. He wore a formal dress coat, with a tie, and had a meticulously trimmed, red-brown beard. Since that first day at Cormon's, he had let his beard grow. In the portrait, a dark, felt bowler hat sat toward the back of his head. His piercing eyes looked straight ahead at the viewer.

"You look so distinguished, like a banker or a politician."

"Let me show you my latest work." He walked her into his bedroom, where she noticed a covered canvas sitting on the easel in the corner of the room.

"What is that, a work in progress?"

Vincent went over to the easel, moved it into the center of the room, and removed the cloth from the canvas. "I'm still working on this study."

Agostina gazed at the painting of a large, white tambourine that held a flood of yellow and dark purple pansies. She whispered, "Vincent, it's beautiful."

"You can have it for the walls of your Café du Tambourin."

"No, I can't accept such a gift."

"Agostina, I insist. I painted it for you."

Agostina took off her shoes and sat down in silence on the unmade bed. She sipped her drink and seemed to drift off into quiet contemplation.

Van Gogh knew what she was thinking. "I am Vincent. Please look upon me as a different person, someone other than my brother."

She put her drink down on a side table and moved toward him. He sat on the bed and embraced her forcefully, pulling her body closer. He kissed her on the neck.

Vincent stood up from the bed. "I'll be right back. Don't move." He walked into the living room, where he fixed himself another drink, and locked the door to the apartment.

When he got back to the bedroom, Agostina was nude on the rumpled bedspread, and the light tone of her derriere stood out against her olive skin. She was resting on her right side, and her body looked like a meandering stream. Starting at her bare feet, Vincent's eyes traveled up to her bent knees, and then turned and came down to her buttocks. He followed the curve up her back and the wide braid of hair that led to her head. She was turned toward the wall. The pose made her look like the most sensuous model Vincent could ever paint. But this was not the time for brushes and perspective. Vincent sat on the bed and took off his clothes.

Like he was disturbing a marvelous painting, he turned Agostina toward him. Her soft, ample bosom bounced as she turned her body. He kissed her lips and her eyes. Taking her breasts in his hands, she squeezed the nipples between his fingers. She then began kissing Vincent on his neck and chest and went down beneath his abdomen. She treated him to the pleasures of her mouth. As she sensed his rising passion, she moved back on the bed, and he entered her vagina.

The artist made love with such force and energy that Agostina was overwhelmed. Responding to his ardent lovemaking, the former model whispered, "You feel marvelous, Vincent. Love me all night."

23

Much later that night, they entered Agostina's flat on Rue de Douai, around the corner from Le Tambourin. Agostina's mother had fallen fast asleep on the love seat in the front parlor, where she had tried to stay awake.

After Agostina gently awakened her mother, Vincent introduced himself to the elderly woman. But tonight, she only spoke Italian and only to her daughter. Speaking excitedly, she admonished her daughter for not informing her of the evening's plans. With that, she turned and left the parlor for her bedroom. Agostina looked like a little girl as she smiled at Vincent, shrugged her shoulders, and held up her hands.

Vincent smiled back through tired eyes. Kissing the woman's hand, he said, "It's time I returned to my bed. There's the atelier in a few hours."

"When will I see you again?" asked Agostina.

"Would you like to go to the Moulin de la Galette on Sunday?"

"Yes, that would be wonderful."

As he walked back toward his apartment, the artist passed many of the bistros and brasseries that he had been frequenting since arriving in Montmartre. He thought about the great friends he was making at the atelier and at these establishments, which were boarded closed for the night. At this late hour, the only light was provided by gaslights on poles and facades of buildings.

It was even too late for the disreputable. However, in the shadows, he did spot a few streetwalkers standing in an alleyway looking out for the police of the Morals Brigade. It was past the time prostitutes were allowed on the street.

Even though prostitution was an accepted part of the life of a young man, Vincent never felt right about it. He came from a very strict Protestant upbringing and frequented prostitutes out of necessity and not choice. It appeared that the artist could never establish a lasting relationship with an acceptable young woman. Things never quite worked out.

As he walked through the dark streets, he remembered his two-year relationship with Clasina Maria Hoornik and her two children in The Hague. He tried to convert the woman, whom he called "Sien," from the life of prostitution by supporting her on the allowance he received from his family. Vincent's relatives, particularly his father, were very upset with his choice of a companion. This was also about the time that Vincent decided he would become an artist. He used the woman and her children as models for his drawings of rural peasants.

Finally, Sien went back to prostitution, even though van Gogh treated her and her children like his family. Vincent could not live with the betrayal and left her. Ironically, for many years later, he felt as if he had betrayed her and the children, for he was their only hope for survival. By then, his art had become his religion and the essence of his life. He told himself that he no longer had the inclination for personal relationships. Later, Sien would take her own life by drowning herself in the river Scheldt.

That was before Agostina. Tonight, he felt like a naive schoolboy. Van Gogh was smitten. He felt that, after long last, he actually had a socially acceptable woman in his life. He could now become an accepted member of civilized society, a part of the reputable community of Paris. Cocottes were not needed anymore; he finally had a good woman.

24

Strolling up the steep walkway, Agostina held Vincent's arm as they climbed the butte to La Moulin de la Galettes. It was a warm, beautiful Sunday afternoon in late July, and they could see the windmills on top of the hill. Vincent wore his brother's straw hat and a brown three-piece suit, while Agostina was clad in a black dress of layered lace with matching bonnet. Along the slope of the hill, white daisies and tall, yellow sunflowers bore further witness to the long days of summer.

The Moulin, their destination, was actually two windmills, one of which was still used to grind lily bulbs for the eventual manufacture of perfume. Every Sunday, starting in the spring, Montmartre families, students, and artists gathered here to dance, drink, and have fun. It was an open-air café-concert with a large dance floor and a stage holding an orchestra. The mill was famous for its flat pancakes, called *galettes*, heated and spiced with cinnamon to complement the mulled wine.

"Vincent, did you ever hear about the *histoire* of the Debray family, the owners of the mill?" asked Agostina, as they approached the entrance to the Moulin.

"No, what happened?"

"Well, locals tell the story of the invasion of Russian Cossacks in 1814. Monsieur Debray tried to defend the mill from the invaders but was killed. The enemy tied his bloody corpse to one of the windmill's wings and let it revolve in the prevailing wind. The Russians warned the family not to touch the body. But in the night, Madame Debray cut her husband down and hastily buried him in a cemetery near the mill. Fortunately, the Cossacks did not return."

"That's an amazing story," said Vincent, "considering that today the Moulin is such a happy place."

"Fifty centimes per couple, monsieur," said the young man standing in the booth alongside the entrance to the Moulin. The artist paid the admission and took Agostina's hand as they passed through the gate. They were immediately caught up in the music, laughter, and singing. On the dance floor, they could see about forty couples waltzing to the stimulating music. The dancing area was surrounded by rows of picnic tables and benches full of cheerful but well-dressed adults and children.

"Tina, can you find either Henri or Emile in this crowd?"

"No, I cannot see them … are they with anyone else?"

"Well, I believe Henri is with his girlfriend, Suzanne. She's an artists' model who also wants to be a painter."

A loud, resonant voice broke through the music and laughter. "Vincent, over here! We're sitting in the shade!"

The Dutchman turned away from the dance floor and saw his friends sitting in the back row close to the trees. Henri and Suzanne were sitting across the table from Emile. Between them sat a plate of galettes and a full carafe of mulled wine.

"Vincent, we've been saving you a place," said Emile. "Come, you and Agostina sit here next to me."

As they slid between the bench and table, Henri stood. "Agostina Segatori, I would like to introduce my friend, Mademoiselle Suzanne Valadon. You'll be seeing that name in the Louvre. She's just starting to paint, but she has great talent."

"Agostina, I'm very pleased to meet you. And don't listen to Henri. I've got much to learn about painting."

Still standing, van Gogh offered, "Suzanne, Agostina is the owner of Café du Tambourin."

"It is an honor to meet the famous *L'Italienne de Montparnasse*," answered Suzanne. When I first came to Paris, you were a legend modeling for Corot, Gerome, Courbet, and Manet. I'm a model also, and I could not hope to work for artists of that caliber."

Lautrec quickly chimed in. "My dear, you happen to be in the company of three of the greatest artists in Montmartre. Your continued association can only bring you prestige and fame."

Everyone laughed, including Vincent, who did not realize the extent of Agostina's reputation in the Parisian art scene.

Suzanne added, "You were also the margouin for *Woman with a Tambourine*, one of Jean-Baptiste Corot's greatest portraits?"

"Is that how you were inspired to pick the name for your café?" asked Vincent.

"It gave me the idea, but I chose the name because the tambourine had been a symbol of female defiance against male domination for centuries. The Semitic harlots of the Temple of Ishtar used the tambourine to celebrate a woman's right to self-determination. It was the symbol of the independent mistress."

"I believe you are in the company of another independent woman, my boys," gloated Suzanne.

Emile then asked, "Of course, you are the Agostina from the Corot painting of the same title?"

"Oui, it was I, but let's change the subject. You're making me feel as if I should be in the dusty, old Louvre alongside the *Venus de Milo.*"

"Bernard, you should find a dancing partner in this sea of young girls," said Henri, to change the subject.

"Oh, there are many young women here, but the good girls are not permitted to dance with strangers. Their parents watch them like the gendarme."

"Well, you may dance with me, Emile," said Suzanne. "Henri, is that acceptable to you?"

"Why of course, Suzanne. Emile is my official substitute. I do all his drinking, and he does all my dancing."

Emile was bursting with pride as he escorted Suzanne toward the dance floor. She was radiant in her afternoon dress of brown-and-lavender-striped satin with a bustle. A matching pink-and-brown chiffon hat held a sprig of small, white flowers. The young man was thankful for the dancing lessons his parents had recently forced him to endure.

"They make a handsome couple," said Lautrec as everyone watched the dancers spinning to a waltz by Chopin.

"She's a very beautiful girl, Henri," said Agostina. "How long have you known her?"

"Suzanne's been with me for four months. It's the longest affair I've ever had in my life. But how long can such a beautiful, vibrant girl be content with me. I cannot even dance with her."

"Oh no, Monsieur Henri," protested Agostina, "you make a wonderful beau. A woman is looking for more in life than a good dancer. You are charming and talented, and the ladies love to be with you. You're the kind of man who makes a good husband."

"Oh, my dear, you are so kind, if it was only that easy. People want to be with me, but I can't stand to be with myself. When I'm alone, I am either working or drinking, or both."

Van Gogh chimed in. "God, this sounds like my life. Didn't we come here to have a good time and get away from the raging beast of work?"

"Vincent, try these galettes," said Agostina. "And drink some mulled wine … you'll like the spices."

The three raised their filled glasses and toasted the fallen heroes of Montmartre. On the dance floor, Emile and Suzanne were enjoying each other's company. A trained dancer from her days in the circus, Suzanne had the ability to anticipate the music while still following her partner's lead.

When the music ended, the orchestra started to play a slow, popular ballad. The couple stayed together, and Emile held her tighter, leading her into the changing melody.

"How long have you been an artist, Emile?"

"It seems like all my life, nearly nineteen years. But I feel as if my life has just started. I've come to realize that beauty exists everywhere, and for the artist it is just a matter of recognizing and capturing it."

"Oui," said Suzanne, "many artists never find the right subject to paint. They might have the skill but do not know how to direct their talents."

"My father wants me to stop painting and join the family business. But Grandmama loves my art and recently had a wooden studio constructed for me near my parent's home in Asnieres."

"That's very moving. Your grandmother sounds like a very sensitive woman who loves her grandson."

Emile caught a trace of a tear along the surface of Suzanne's green eyes. Embarrassed, she broke from his gaze. "I think we should get back."

Returning to the table was no easy matter. Many more people were walking toward the dance floor and milling about. Emile took Suzanne by the hand to lead her through the throngs of people standing among the rows of tables.

"Ah, the two love birds have finally returned to the nest," said Henri. "Are you two enjoying yourselves?"

"Yes, we are. Emile is a good dancer. He's easy to follow."

"Well, you certainly couldn't follow me. My cane would get in the way. Emile's a tall, strong young man and quite handsome. Don't you think Emile is handsome, Suzanne?"

"Henri, don't do this ..."

"Just answer the question, Suzanne. Is Emile handsome? *Oui ou non?*"

Emile interrupted. "Henri, it was just a dance, and you said it was all right."

"Piss off, Emile. I'm not talking to you."

Vincent was getting very upset by the confrontation. It reminded him of all the fights he had endured with members of his own family.

"Please, no more of this," said van Gogh. "Henri, this warm wine is going to your head. Let's fight about art as we always do. It's more predictable."

Despite a lull in the conversation, Emile felt his presence was making everyone uncomfortable. To prevent further embarrassment, he stepped back from the table and dropped his head. "Mademoiselles Suzanne, Agostina, gentlemen, it is getting late. I'm going back down the butte. Adieu."

With that, Emile grabbed his straw hat from the bench, put it on his head, and walked away through the music and gaiety of the afternoon. After Emile was out of sight, Vincent was the first to speak. "Henri, the young fellow didn't do anything wrong."

"I did not say he did. I just made the observation that Emile and Suzanne looked like a happy and handsome couple."

"Suzanne, would you be so kind as to show me the location of the ladies' water closet?" asked Agostina.

"Oui, come with me. I believe it's over behind the stage."

When the ladies were gone, Vincent looked over at Henri. "What the hell are you trying to do, make this the longest afternoon since the Cossacks attacked the Moulin? You sound like a fucking bore."

"Gogh, whom am I kidding? Watching Suzanne with someone else made me realize that she couldn't possibly love me for long. I know Emile is too young for Suzanne, but I can see the way you look at her, Vincent. Why don't you take her off my hands?"

"Henri, you can't be serious."

"I'm perfectly serious. Since our first time together, Suzanne has made me feel more and more inadequate. She also disappears for days at a time. I fear she's sleeping with other men."

"How can you say that?"

"Because these women are all the same. Do you think that Agostina is a Carmelite nun? That cabaret she operates is actually a *café de femmes*, an unlicensed establishment where men pay the waitresses and get laid."

"How could that be? Would not the police shut it down?"

"Here's the good part. Your little Tina is able to operate it without a license because she sleeps with a police prefect."

"How could that be? I always thought she was a moral person operating a legitimate business."

"Vincent, don't take it so hard. You've been here long enough to know that Montmarte and morality do not get along together."

Van Gogh then realized he knew very little about his new lover. He anticipated confronting Agostina to get her side of the story.

Standing in front of the wall mirror in the ladies water closet, Suzanne was fixing her hair and repositioning her hat.

"Agostina, I don't know what's happening between me and Henri. When we first started the affair, I felt he loved me. But every time we're together, I feel less love and affection from him. He's more short-tempered and claims it's me who's changed."

"Suzanne, lovers see what they want to. Everyone has imperfections, but thinking the other person is dwelling on our shortcomings can destroy a relationship. Henri is a very complex man. I don't have to tell you that."

"Agostina, I do not believe that Henri is capable of loving one woman for more than a short time."

"You may be right. He appears to sabotage his own happiness."

As the two couples walked slowly down the butte from La Moulin de la Galettes, Vincent looked at Agostina in a different way. He had so many questions to ask her about the café, but he did not care to confront her in the presence of the other couple.

From all the mulled wine and galettes, Henri was having a difficult time traversing the walkway down the hill. He had to stop and rest along the path. Van Gogh also looked at the little count in a new light. Sympathy was always obscured by Henri's vitality and enthusiasm. But his inability to love Suzanne, or any woman, made Vincent feel very sad for his friend.

25

After saying good-bye to Suzanne and Henri on Rue Lepic, Agostina followed van Gogh through the wooden doors and into the entrance to his flat. As they climbed to the third floor, Vincent did not say a word, even though distressing questions percolated in his mind.

As they arrived at the front door, they were greeted by Theo, who quickly excused himself and retired to his room. He knew his brother was dating Agostina, and he wanted to give the couple some privacy. Agostina walked into Vincent's room, took off her bonnet, and lay on the bed.

"What's wrong, Vincent? You seem very quiet since we left the Moulin?"

"I've learned something today that you must explain to me."

"What, what is it?"

Grabbing Agostina's arm, the Dutchman yelled, "Is that café of yours a café de femmes, a fucking bordello?"

"Grow up, you crude innocent,"said Agostina, pulling her arm away. "I thought you knew. Most bistros and cafés along the boulevard sell our waitresses the way we sell our food and drinks."

"And what about your protector, the police prefect? Do you deny that you sleep with him so you can operate a bordello without a license?"

"You sanctimonious hypocrite," she answered with tears forming in her eyes. "It's impossible for a woman to run a business today in Montmartre without people to help her."

Shaking with rage, Van Gogh shouted, "So, you admit it. You sleep with me and with this crooked gendarme at the same time."

"So, so what? Do you want me to go to confession at Abbey de Saint Dennis? I do what I must to survive."

"Agostina, tonight I was ready to ask you to marry me, and I find out from Henri that you deceive me behind my back."

"What's wrong with you? I'm not interested in marriage. I'm here because I want to be here. Do you want to screw or not?"

The Dutchman was still angry but was surprised by Agostina's crude offer. Suddenly, he felt her unbridled sexuality and knew that he had to have her again.

"Tina, I'm sorry ... I desire you more than ever."

Vincent lay down on the bed beside her, kissing her heavily on the mouth through her salty tears. He then helped Agostina out of her black lace dress, underwear, and black stockings. When she was naked, he quickly removed his own clothes and continued kissing her and stroking her body. Their lovemaking took on a ferocious intimacy that lasted for the rest of the evening, until both lay exhausted.

In the darkness, the artist reached out for Agostina, whispering, "Tina, I do not care what you have done. I love you and still want to marry you."

After a long pause, she answered, "No, I don't want to marry you or anyone. Marriage in this day and age is like going into a trap and forfeiting your freedom. Besides, who will earn the living? You're still finding your way in your art career."

"Please, Tina, I'll make a good husband. You'll see."

"No, Vincent. I'll continue to see you, but let us not have any more talk of marriage."

26

Overlooking the windmills of Moulin de la Gallete, high on the butte, Emile and Vincent were laden with painting materials. On their backs, they carried folded tripod easels tied horizontally to wooden backpacks. Under their arms were blank canvases primed for oil painting.

"This is a fine spot," said Vincent. "We can see both the Moulin and the vegetable gardens."

"Yes, but the sun is directly overhead, and it promises to become another hot afternoon."

"Do not concern yourself, my boy. I welcome the heat on my face. It cooks my brain and brings out things that I cannot see. After all, sunshine is a gift from God."

Vincent's canvas was a large rectangle almost four feet across. With a metal hammer that he carried in his belt, he drove the three legs of the lightweight easel into the ground to stabilize the canvas.

With a crayon, he marked off a space about twelve inches wide in the upper-right corner of the canvas. After preparing his colors and brushes, he started to sketch and paint only in the small section outlined by the crayon. He depicted the walkway and wooden bleachers where sightseers sat to watch the festivities at the Moulin and get a view of the distant skyline of Paris.

Emile Bernard, whose easel was turned in the opposite direction, began painting a scene of windmills and rows of vegetables and colorful wildflowers. After a short while, he turned to the other painter and asked, "Do you believe in God?"

"I can do without a benevolent deity in my life and in my painting, but I do think that sunshine is a gift from God," answered Van Gogh, still working on his painting.

"But don't we all need a higher force in our lives, a creator who gives meaning to our lives?"

"Yes, that higher force, or God, is in my capacity to create," said Vincent as he turned to face Emile. "Indeed, it is bigger than myself. I no longer look for God in churches. Christ is more of an artist than anyone. He works in the spirit and the living flesh. He creates men not statues."

Looking into Vincent's eyes, Emile asked, "But aren't you afraid of dying?"

"No, even though I feel that I don't have many years left. I would, however, like to create that one great painting that everyone will hail as a masterpiece. I don't have much time."

"Don't be such a pessimist. You have a long life ahead of you, with a lot more women and absinthe."

After completing a small painting in the upper corner of the canvas, Vincent moved his easel and focused his attention on the little farms and windmills. He started a second painting in the bottom-right corner of the canvas.

By the end of the day, the large canvas looked like a little museum. There were no less than six small paintings on the single canvas. Later, Van Gogh could cut them apart and frame them individually. A light, Impressionistic style with little detail characterized each painting. Most demonstrated a wide mixture of bright colors. Vincent's palette was no longer reflective of the somber tones of Rembrandt and the early Dutch masters. He was a modern painter experimenting with both the French and Japanese influences around him.

As the afternoon's brightness retreated into the fading light of evening, the two artists started to collect their materials. With their easels folded and strapped to their backpacks, they carried their wet canvases down the walkway past the Moulin de la Galettes to the walkway leading down the butte of Montmartre.

As the painters walked down a flight of steps, they spotted a large group of men sitting below. It was an apache gang, a group of young ruffians.

When the gang's leader noticed the difference in ages between Emile and Vincent, he cried out, "What do we have here, an old faggot and his paramour?"

One of the other young men grabbed a canvas out of Emile's hands. "Let's see what you two homos have been up to."

Emile was afraid, but he protested. "Give me back the painting. The paint is still wet."

The apache moved the painting further away from Bernard. "Yeah, you're wet, all right … wet between the legs." The men laughed.

Vincent dropped his canvas on its back and said, "Give back the painting, and leave us alone!"

"Look, papa, we'll leave you after you hand over your francs. All your money, or we'll beat the fucking hell out of both of you."

The artists were now surrounded by the gang, which totaled about ten young men. Tearing off his own backpack, Vincent told Emile to stand behind him. After grabbing the hammer from his belt, he quickly struck the side of the leader's head. The young man fell onto the sidewalk, yelling in pain. The Dutchman then swung the hammer savagely in the opposite direction, hitting another gang member. The rest of the gang tore after Vincent, but he forced them back by wildly swinging the hammer.

The men then grabbed hold of Emile and started punching and kicking him. Vincent threw the hammer, which hit one of Emile's attackers in the face. He then bent down and pulled the wooden easel from his backpack. Holding it as a weapon, he swung it like the wing of a windmill. The metal junction of the tripod hit three or four of the men, showering the sidewalk with droplets of blood.

From the bottom of the hill Vincent heard a police whistle and men shouting. The apaches, bruised and bleeding, ran up the stairs like frightened rabbits. Only their leader was left behind. He lay on the sidewalk, holding his bleeding head in his hands.

Vincent ran over to Emile and was checking him for injuries when the gendarme arrived. One of the policemen, seeing Vincent comforting his friend, declared, "What do we have here? A faggot and his bruised lover?"

Vincent did not answer, at first. But when he saw that Emile was not seriously hurt, he stood up and addressed the gendarme. "You fuck, we're painters, and those men just attacked us for our money!"

"What did you call me, you faggot?"

Vincent was covered with droplets of blood, which mixed with the paint on his shirt. His green eyes looked at the policeman with such intensity that the man put his hand on his pistol. The other gendarme, who had a cooler head than his partner, declared, "Let's all calm down. You men have been through a violent experience."

Emile ran over to his friend. "Come, Vincent, let's get our things together and leave."

"Not so fast. There's an injured man here," said the policeman, still touching his gun. "I want everyone to come to the police precinct. We must write a complete report."

The men were taken to the office of Auguste Mignotte, the prefect of the Morals Brigade for the Montmartre section. The first officer on the scene had decided to treat the incident not as an attempted robbery but as a morals crime involving homosexuals. Mignotte was a large man with broad shoulders, an enormous bald head, and a small square mustache. He looked over the folder and read the report. "So, the scene was covered with blood, and you two gentlemen don't have a scratch on you? My gendarmes say the gang that accosted you had almost a dozen young apaches. How did you put up a fight against those odds?"

Van Gogh became angry.

Emile answered in a dignified tone. "Prefect, we are art students who did not do anything wrong. My colleague, Monsieur van Gogh, fought back with everything at his disposal. We were just fortunate that your gendarmes arrived."

"It sounds like it was lucky for the apaches. This Dutchman could be a menace to peaceful French society."

Vincent started to say something, but Emile interrupted. "Please, Cent, let's just be quiet."

Mignotte stepped back from the two men. "All right, we're going to let you go, but if there's any more trouble from either of you, you will regret it. Van Gogh, France is an open country, but you're still considered a foreigner. You can be deported. So, keep your nose clean."

Vincent listened to Mignotte but still felt like a nervous animal about to attack for his own survival.

"Come on, Gogh. Let's get our paintings and get out of here. I assure you, prefect, we shan't be back here again."

27

As the affair with Agostina continued, van Gogh seemed to intensify the search for his own creative style. Like a bee visiting as many flowers as possible, van Gogh tried to expose himself to every type of artistic technique and medium throughout the Parisian art world.

Most of the painters he met were classic Impressionists, who used pure, strong colors to describe the fleeting moment. Many, like van Gogh, were influenced by the new Japanese prints with their asymmetry, spatial dynamics, and the use of two-dimensional surfaces. Blending the Impressionist style with the Japanese was a challenge not easily mastered.

One afternoon, Vincent dropped in at his brother's gallery office.

"Theo, do you have an inexpensive print of an Impressionist painting that I could use as a *maquette*—a model. I want to experiment with the Impressionists' technique."

"Yes, you can have this paper reproduction of Claude Monet's *Tulip fields of Amsterdam.*"

Like a man with a compulsion, Vincent rushed back to Boulevard de Clichy and Cormon's atelier with the rolled up print in his hand. This afternoon, the studio was nearly empty, as most of the students were working on outside projects. He unrolled the print and tacked it up on an empty easel near his chair.

After placing a medium-sized, blank canvas on his own easel, he prepared the oils that corresponded to the colors in the Monet painting. Studying the details of the Monet, he was struck by the lack of draftsmanship. A giant windmill dominated a large field of colorful tulips that ran to a river in the distance, with the city of Amsterdam on the far horizon. The windmill possessed its general shape but was painted hurriedly, without the aid of a charcoal outline or pencil drawing. Up to that time, van Gogh always used a detailed charcoal drawing before applying his paints. But now, he wanted to see and think as an Impressionist.

Without painting a background, he coated a small, flat brush with dark brown color and attempted to paint his own impression of the windmill. He copied the dark shape of the mill and its roof and then added the crossing wings of the structure. After painting a gray horizon across the painting, he took a round brush and started to copy the numerous tulips that Monet had put into his painting. To van

Gogh's consternation, Monet had also created the flowers without a guiding drawing but utilized the mingling of colors and their hues. Very precisely, he tried to copy a few of the large tulips in the foreground, but they did not look anything like Monet's flowers. The smaller tulips in the distance were even harder to duplicate. After about an hour of total concentration, Vincent was both frustrated and exhausted.

Louis Anquetin walked into the room just in time to see Vincent about to throw the wet canvas across the room. "Hold it there, Vincent. These walls are spattered enough with droplets of our work. Let me see what has you so upset."

"Louis, this is impossible. I'm no Impressionist. I'm not even an artist. I tried to copy Monet's view of a tulip field, and all I have here is a fucking mess."

"That's because Impressionism and, for that matter, Japonisme are not based on form and detail but on color, light, and mood. One cannot just change from traditional academic painting to Impressionism overnight. It takes years, and you have to look at things totally differently. Actually, a trick many Impressionists utilize is to squint at a scene with their eyes half closed. It isolates the shapes and gives you a good idea of tonal qualities."

"But my tendency is to express realism and detail in what I see. Louis, I worked for a long time with a gray, somber palette. The use of bright, vibrant color was never part of my vision."

"I had the same difficulty, and my first instructor, Professeur Dumont, told me that the best way to develop a facility with color is by studying the interplay of light on flowers and plants. He had me paint cut flowers for many months."

28

Vincent took Louis Anquetin's suggestion to heart and started to paint flowers in still life to obtain a grasp of color and to capture the fleeting moment of Impressionism. During the subsequent weeks, painting flowers became an obsession to van Gogh.

Many of his fellow art students at Cormon's atelier took an abiding interest in Vincent's progress. They would often bring cut flowers to him before class in the morning.

But perhaps, the most profound metamorphosis of van Gogh as an artist arose from an unlikely source. One afternoon, he returned to the flat shared on Rue Lepic and found a large wooden packing crate. Apparently, it had been delivered to the flat during the day. The box was addressed to Theo and had been sent from Marseilles.

The puzzled artist walked around the box several times. He tried to figure out what was inside by picking it up and gently shaking it. He surmised it was artwork, such as paintings or a sculpture.

Just as he could stand it no longer, his brother returned from his day at the gallery.

"Ah, I see you have discovered the box from Marseilles!" exclaimed Theo as he removed his hat and looked around for tools to open the crate.

"What is in here, Theo? I cannot imagine."

"Well, when I was away in Marseilles this last time, I came upon the most outstanding paintings by an artist who had just passed away."

"What is the name of this painter?"

Theo pulled the nails out of the wooden crate. "His name was Adolphe Joseph Monticelli. He died earlier this year, destitute and penniless."

As he freed the six paintings from the crate, Theo asked Vincent to stand back and view the studies from across the room. Vincent observed that Monticelli used richly textured and colored surfaces to produce a dazzling effect. Thick, heavy dabs of impasto paint, some applied right from the tube, gave the landscapes and still lifes an almost three-dimensional quality. Vincent felt that Monticelli was heavily influenced by Eugene Delacroix's arrangement of complementary colors in his works.

Adolphe Joseph Thomas Monticelli was a French painter of the generation preceding the Impressionists. He was born in Marseille in 1824 in humble circumstances but was admitted to the Ecole des Beaux-Arts in Paris, where he studied under Paul Delaroche. While in Paris, he developed a highly unique and instinctive style of painting. After 1870, Monticelli returned to Marseille and lived in poverty. He sold many of his paintings for meager sums—often just enough for food and drink.

Monticelli also experimented with the discoveries of the Impressionists but did not feel comfortable with the style. Similar to van Gogh, he was also an unworldly man who dedicated himself exclusively to his art.

"Theo, look at the effect of the light on the dabs of paint. There's actually a shadow produced by the thick paint. Monticelli is more of a sculptor than a painter."

"So, you are impressed by my new acquisitions?"

"Theo, this is almost like a spiritual experience. I feel like I've known this painter from a former life."

"Well, he was a good friend of Paul Cézanne when Paul was young. They painted landscapes together while roaming the Aix countryside in the south of France."

"Theo, this painter sees flowers and nature just as I do. You can also feel the essence of the subjects in his canvases. Monticelli's colors come from his gut, from his emotions. If I could only paint like that ..."

"Why don't you try? It's only a matter of thinking like Monticelli."

29

During the following morning, as van Gogh entered the hallway that led to Cormon's atelier, he sensed that something was different. Several of his fellow students, including Louis Anquetin, were standing in front of a large paper sign that was tacked up on an easel. It read:

Until further notice, this atelier is closed for renovations. All students should remove their personal equipment and supplies from their workstations. In addition, students will please remove their artwork, irrespective of the stage of completion. Students have until 3:00 PM tomorrow, 27 August, 1886, to conform to this request, at which time all remaining materials will be disposed of. After renovations are complete, the status of all students will be reexamined and those selected will be asked to rejoin the atelier.

Fernand Cormon, Directeur

"What's the meaning of this, Louis?" asked van Gogh. "Is Cormon out of his mind?"

"No, Vincent, this has been coming for some time. Cormon has been complaining that the discipline in the classes and the lack of respect for the instructors have become unbearable."

"Cormon, I'll murder that bastard!" yelled van Gogh. "I trust that he is closing the atelier to reopen it again to get rid of the undesirables, like me." Van Gogh took the atelier closing as a personal attack against him and his behavior.

"It's not just you," said Louis. "Even Henri has had a falling out with Cormon."

"Well, I was getting tired of this atelier, anyway. I can experiment with my colors on my own. I've got all the great painters of Montmartre to advise me."

Van Gogh entered the atelier and started to pack up his canvases and art supplies. He carried the first of several armfuls of materials across the street to Le Tambourin.

As the artist came into the front door of the café, Agostina was standing there. "What's all this? This is a café, not a studio."

"It's okay, Tina. I just have to store these things here for a short time. Cormon has closed the teaching atelier. In the next trip, I'll bring my still-life paintings of flowers. You may hang them on the walls to decorate the café."

After Vincent had carried all of his materials across the street, he presented Agostina with four canvases of colorful flowers. The flowers, which included gladioli, lilacs, poppies, peonies, and zinnias, were depicted in vases that complemented the flowers' colors.

Agostina was quite impressed. "These are magnifique! They shall bring a light and airy feeling into this drab café."

"You can have them in payment for free meals and drink. What do you say?"

"No, my dear. These painting are yours. If we sell some to our customers, then we can negotiate."

As van Gogh and Agostina continued their discussion, the bar filled up with many of the students from Cormon's atelier, including Louis and Henri. After all, this was Paris, where many brasseries and cafés open to serve alcohol in the morning.

As the café became crowded, Vincent noticed a large man with a black hat and a small moustache standing all alone at the far corner of the bar. He seemed to fill the space like he owned it. Finally, the man removed his hat and placed it on the bar. When the gaslight from above bathed his face, Vincent recognized Police Prefect Mignotte from the Morals Brigade. The Dutchman realized this was the man extorting Agostina.

Mignotte never forgot a face. He remembered van Gogh from the episode with the apache gang.

When their eyes met, Vincent ran past the other artists at the bar and confronted Mignotte. "Get out of here, you crooked bastard, or I'll kill you!"

"What are you talking about, you crazed Dutchman? In this country, you don't threaten the police or interfere with police business."

"Look, Mignotte, Agostina is a good woman. You leave her be."

"You little worm, I've got a good mind to put your girlfriend into the women's prison at Saint-Lazar and jail you until we can deport you back to the Netherlands."

It was too late for calm. The artist reached back and was about to deliver a roundhouse fist to Mignotte's face when Louis Anquetin grabbed Vincent's arm, and Henri ran in between the two men to keep them apart. Mignotte reached for his police revolver. The rest of the artists jumped on Vincent and dragged him kicking and screaming out of the front door of the café.

Out on the street, Henri was the first to speak. "Now, just calm down, Gogh. That man would have shot you. There's not much you can do right now, but let me handle this. I'll come up with something."

"Mignotte is the policeman who screws her. I don't care what they do to me. I still want to kill him."

"No, no more such talk," said Louis. "Let's go down the boulevard and have a drink and some food to get your attention off this Mignotte character."

Escaping the circle of young men surrounding him, van Gogh walked slowly away from Café du Tambourin. He looked forward to a drink of absinthe, raide.

30

The next morning, Julien Tanguy and his wife were engaged in their usual bickering when Vincent entered the paint shop on Rue Clauzel. Tanguy got the last word and broke from the exchange to greet the artist with an eager smile. "Bonjour, today is my big day. You are here to paint my portrait."

"Oui, monsieur, just let me set up my things. But Julien, don't let me interfere with your work. Just stay seated on your stool."

Madame Tanguy, who did not share her husband's fascination for art or artists, left the shop for the living quarters.

Van Gogh set up his easel directly in front of Tanguy. He placed eight large and colorful Japanese prints on the wall directly behind his model. Tanguy was also asked to briefly put on his straw hat and double-breasted blue jacket, which van Gogh quickly sketched onto the painting.

"Clasp your hands together in your lap, with the back of one hand covering the other hand's fingers."

Vincent knew exactly what he wanted the painting to look like. He desired to capture the old man's calm serenity and to accomplish this in a synthesis of Japanese and French-Impressionistic art. He worked without any hesitation. He did not want his intellect to correct his emotions.

The artist deliberately omitted portions of the eight colorful prints that hung behind Tanguy, so the background of his painting only showed parts of them. The Japanese prints were all very colorful, but they contrasted with Vincent's main figure. He used dabs and lines of green, red, blue, tan, and brown to capture the man's rough features and mild personality. The white sparkle in the old man's blue eyes showed his spirit and vitality.

During the course of the morning, a few artists came into the shop to purchase supplies. When the old man left the scene to take care of his customers, Vincent would concentrate on the background Japonisme until Tanguy reappeared.

By noon, the painting was complete. Within minutes after twelve, the front door opened, and in walked a gloomy, nasty-looking man in his forties with a strong Southern accent. The man looked at van Gogh and then at the freshly painted work on the easel. He did not say a word.

"Ah, *bonjour*, Monsieur Cézanne," said Tanguy. "This is Vincent van Gogh. He's painting my portrait."

"Is that what this is?" answered Cézanne. "Monsieur, you really paint like a madman."

Unpredictably, Vincent did not react. He was pleased with his painting, and that was all that mattered. The Dutchman also realized that he had met Paul Cézanne once before in the mezzanine of Theo's gallery. Apparently, Cézanne was too self-centered to remember.

After Cézanne left the shop, Vincent packed up his easel and materials and handed the portrait to Tanguy. "Here, père, put this in your front window. You come up with a fair price, and if it sells, you keep half."

"You know, Vincent, your palette gets lighter and more colorful every month. I like this better than all the other paintings you have brought me."

As Tanguy put the painting in the front window, the front door opened again. The imposing Paul Gauguin, with his broad frame and striking red face, appeared.

"Paul, what are you doing here?" said Vincent. "I thought you were back in Brittany by now."

"No, I'm still painting around Paris, for the weather has been superb."

"Then, Paul, come with us. Emile and I are going to paint this afternoon in Asnieres, by way of Clichy. Join us."

"That sounds *splendide*. Let me get a few colors and brushes, and we shall be on our way."

Tanguy got together all the materials that Gauguin requested. When he started to slowly put his change together to pay for the supplies, Julien said, "Forget it, comrade. You can pay me next week."

Having overheard her husband's words, Madame Tanguy reappeared. She removed her apron, threw it on the floor, and walked out of the shop, saying, "You are hopeless, Julien. When will you stop giving these painters our life's bread?"

Laden with portable easels and art supplies, Vincent, Paul, and Emile made their way up Boulevard de Clichy, through the town of Clichy, and toward the northern village of Asnieres, located about six kilometers from Montmartre. Van Gogh looked like a street cleaner in his blue coveralls, splattered with droplets of paint, and his equipment strapped to his back. For most of the walk, he was way ahead of the other two men, anxious to get to more painting.

They finally reached Pont St. Louis, which leads over the river Seine to the island of St. Louis with Asnieres on its northern bank. From the bridge, Emile pointed out his parents' home in the distance. "After we finish our painting, Mama will have dinner for us, and then we can take the train back to Paris."

"So, that's where you have your private studio and live in the bourgeois lap of luxury," quipped Gauguin.

"You're just jealous," answered Emile. "Evidently, you were raised in the jungle by wolves and savages."

"Well, it's true. I was raised by my Peruvian mother, who was an Inca Indian princess but not a savage. As far as the wolf part is concerned, people say I resemble a wolf. I guess it must be true."

The two other men laughed in reaction to Gauguin's self-deprecating humor. As they continued to walk over the bridge, Paul pointed out another landmark. "There is Jatte Island, the birthplace of the pointillist revolution. It's where Seurat and his colleague Paul Signac spend so much time."

As the painters left the bridge, they made their way down to the river's edge, where they could look upstream, back at the bridge. The artists put down their gear, scouted out their individual vantage points, and set up their easels. Remarkably, the trio was within easy talking distance from one another. Van Gogh instantly composed a picture in his mind's eye—placing the bridge as the focal point, a few small boats in the foreground, and the sky and the distant countryside in the background.

As Gauguin set out the colors of his palette and arranged his brushes, he looked over at the Dutchman. "Just like you, my wife is from the north. She was just like the weather, very cold, but it didn't prevent me from having four kids with her."

"What happened? Is she here in the south with you?" asked van Gogh.

"No, I could not tolerate married life. I like to travel … to see the sights." As he spoke, Gauguin started to work on his painting.

Vincent noticed that he began by blocking out patches of color. Fascinated, he asked, "Gauguin, why no drawing or composition? You compose your study using only the colors to provide the image of the painting."

"That's right, Dutchman. I consider myself a symbolist. It comes from my experience of painting for ceramics. You need definite outlines of color to prevent the mixing of colors during the firing process. I hated the work, but it paid the rent."

"Coloring ceramics contributed to Paul's unique style," added Emile.

Vincent looked confused. "I've always had a problem starting right off with the color."

"That's why the Dutch have not made any advancements in art in two hundred years," said Gauguin. "They are still painting in the old way of Rembrandt."

"If I could paint like Rembrandt," quipped Emile, "I would not be standing out here in the middle of nowhere with two indigent artisans."

The men all laughed, and Gauguin interjected, "I'm not so indigent. Last week, I sold another painting, and your brother Theo has agreed to show my paintings in the mezzanine at Boussod's."

"That's wonderful, Paul," said Emile.

Van Gogh said nothing. He thought about all the paintings he had placed for sale all over Paris without a single buyer. He had them in galleries, cafés, bistros, boutiques, grocery stores, and even a dentist's office. Vincent also remembered that Messieurs Boussod and Valadon, Theo's employers, had made it clear to his brother that they did not want to see any of Vincent's paintings in their gallery. They had known Vincent from the time he was dismissed from the Goupil gallery in the 1870s and always felt he was mentally unstable.

To clear his mind of these negative thoughts, Vincent started to work on his study of the Pont St. Louis over the Seine. Paul startled him by offering some wine, which he had brought from Montmartre. Vincent was most appreciative, and he sipped the red wine from the small, green bottle.

"I see you are conservative with your color, just like the other painters of the north."

"Not everyone is a colorist like you, Paul, using color to tell the story. I try to paint what is there."

"Vincent, I saw your portrait of Tanguy in the shop … and it's a good start. You captured his personality in the colors of his face, but you need to feel the colors not the reality. Reality is not what makes a painting great. Many times, I make up the colors. I hear them rather than see them."

Before van Gogh could respond, the burly painter went back to his own work, leaving the Dutchman to contemplate his words. Van Gogh looked at his painting carefully. As usual, the painting mirrored the reality of the scene. The bridge was accurately drawn with its wooden span and stone supports. The color that van Gogh selected for the water and countryside also reflected what he beheld in his sight.

He remembered Gauguin's words: "I feel the colors, not the reality." After grabbing his palette knife, he mixed more blue into the green, which he had been using for the foliage. The blue reflected the coolness he felt from the wind in his face as it traveled down the river and across the fields. He also added a strong orange hue to the Naples yellow color that he had been using to color the bridge.

The orange brought out the grain of the wood and highlighted the focal point by providing a strong contrast to the cool blue of the water.

He stood back and looked at his work. He liked what he saw. Vincent knew that Gauguin, probably, would approve, but that was not important. The painting of the bridge sang to him. It reminded him of the Japanese prints with their improvised colors and contours, which he had been imitating in the portrait of Tanguy.

Was this the artistic style that would give wings to his soul? He thought, "After all, objects emit emotion, not just people. The sky could be green or brown, just as a face could be red or blue. These are colors far from reality, but they can tell the story of an instant in time."

The men worked on their paintings until early in the evening. Emile then led the two other artists, with their wet canvases and painting materials, to his villa in the hills overlooking the Seine, above the town of Asniers.

Located in an upper-middle-class neighborhood, the villa was protected by a heavy, wooden gate and a shoulder-high stone wall surrounding the house and garden, which included a small vineyard. Alone at the far end of the compound was a small, wooden building with large windows on the north and west sides of the structure.

As the men entered the gate, they were greeted by Emile's mother, Marguerite. She wore an elegant sundress of white cotton and lace. "Bonsoir, messieurs. *Bien-venue.* Emile, did you have a good day?"

"Oui, Mama, it was a grand day for painting."

Emile's father, Francois, quickly appeared. He was wearing the formal attire of a bourgeois gentleman, even though the villa was not located in a large city. With a jovial smile he asked, "Emile, whom have you brought to our home?"

Without waiting for an introduction, the burly artist said, "I am Paul Gauguin, monsieur."

"Ah, Papa, my other friend is Vincent van Gogh. Both men are painters."

Monsieur Bernard extended his hand but changed the expression on his face after hearing of the visitors' occupations.

Sensing the tension, Madame Bernard, a middle-aged woman of aristocratic bearing, added, "Emile, show your friends the grounds and the painter's studio, a gift from my mother." She and her husband then returned to the patio, outside the rear of the house, where they had been drinking their *aperitifs.*

Gauguin looked around the studio. "This is a wonderfully private work space, Emile … much better than the little room we shared in Pont-Aven last year."

Van Gogh was also taken with the studio. "If I had this, I would never leave. Perhaps only to get a fresh supply of absinthe."

As the men strolled the grounds, Vincent asked Gauguin, "Have you ever been to the Café du Tambourin on the boulevard?"

"Why yes, last year before I went to Brittany. I was a steady customer. Who do you think painted those colorful tambourines on the tables?"

"So, you know Agostina, the owner?"

Before Gauguin could answer, Emile interrupted. "I just heard my mother call us to dinner. We're having an early meal so we can catch the train back to the city."

As everyone sat around the table in the villa's dining room, a housekeeper brought out several bottles of red wine and pitchers of water. The table was set with fine silverware and china. A white porcelain vase filled with yellow flowers served as the centerpiece.

The artists, including Emile, were grateful for the home-cooked meal. None had stopped for the midday déjeuner. The wine and chicken, cooked in champagne, with mixed vegetables was an ideal meal for the hungry painters, who had spent the long afternoon in the fresh country air.

During the meal, Francois seemed quite content discussing the ideal weather and the virtues of living in the country. His wife had many questions for her son, asking if he had enough clean clothes and food and if he was taking care of himself.

As everyone had gotten around to the dessert of cheese and fruit, Emile's father turned to van Gogh. "Monsieur, I have a question. You are not a child. You're considerably older than my son. How do you support yourself?"

Vincent put down the fruit he was eating and glared at Emile's father, "I live by my painting, monsieur."

"Oui, but do you make enough money to buy food and lodging, the necessities of life?"

There was a long pause as Vincent gathered his thoughts. "Well, not exactly. My brother has invested in my future. When I begin selling my paintings, I shall be independent."

"Oh, I see, you have not made any money yet. What are you … thirty-six … thirty-seven years old?"

"I'm thirty-four. I do not understand your concern, monsieur. Why are you confronting me?"

"I'll tell you why. My son has taken up this painting nonsense, and he's only nineteen. How long before he makes enough money to support himself?"

Vincent did not answer, for he had heard the same words before from his own father.

Like many parents before him, Monsieur Bernard just continued with his monologue despite the absence of a dialogue. "I want him to come into the family business. We have been manufacturing cloth for generations. The business is booming, and he could have a family, children, and a comfortable life."

"That's all and well, monsieur, but he is happy when he paints."

"Well, I'm happy when I eat a good meal, but I cannot make a living doing that. You painters are wasting the best years of your lives."

The logic was inescapable, but Vincent had heard enough. "You, my good man, are an ignorant, provincial bourgeois who would not recognize art if it bit you in the ass."

No one at the table said anything. A stony silence enveloped the dinner table which was broken by Paul Gauguin's thunderous laugh.

A look of incredulity swept over Francois Bernard's face. In a firm but low voice, he said, "Monsieur van Gogh, I must ask you to leave my home. This is disgraceful."

"Monsieur, you cannot expel me from your house because I am leaving and shall never return."

Emile and his mother tried to calm everyone down but to no avail. Vincent threw down his napkin and ran outside, where he picked up his easel, canvas, and materials. He walked through the gate and headed toward Asniers. It was about ten o'clock, and the evening's summer light was fading into the western sky as Vincent made his way to the railroad station in the center of town.

When he arrived at the small, square station, he found that the next train to Paris would arrive in thirty minutes, so he waited on a bench on the railroad platform.

Vincent's imaginary friend, Willem, appeared sitting on the bench beside him. "So, you really put that son of a bitch in his place. Don't you feel a lot better?"

Vincent turned his head and answered Willem. "No, I don't. The man is right. How long can I go on without selling any paintings? My painting style changes from hour to hour, and my life is getting worse by the day."

"That's right my boy. Pretty soon you'll even lose Agostina," said Willem. "She seems to be retreating into a shell, and she will never be free of Mignotte."

Other passengers started to appear on the platform. They quickly moved away from the bench when they realized that Vincent was having a loud conversation with himself. Everyone was relieved when the train arrived on time. Vincent was back in Montmartre in less than twenty minutes.

31

Vincent continued to see Agostina until his second spring in Montmartre. They never talked about Prefect Mignotte, but the sensitive artist always felt his presence. Agostina was very helpful and encouraging, letting him cover the walls of her café with his paintings and Japanese prints. Van Gogh also held a number of exhibitions with other painters of the Petite Boulevard at Le Tambourin, as well as at other cafés along Boulevard de Clichy. Van Gogh was discouraged when Lautrec, Bernard, and Anquetin sold paintings, while his did not attract any attention.

The day after one of the disappointing exhibitions, Vincent showed up at Café du Tambourin at a little past noon. He had been out almost all night with his fellow artists making the rounds of the cabarets and was quite hung over. Agostina was alone in the café, sitting at one of the round tables that was painted like a large tambourine. She wore a multicolored jacket and a fez from North Africa on her head. She was drinking from a hefty mug of beer, which brought a flush to her cheeks. Her lips were moist, and her eyes sparkled.

"Agostina, you look enchanting. You are glowing like a star. Do not move. I'm going to get my supplies and paint a portrait of you."

As Vincent prepared his paints, Agostina lit a cigarette and struck an interesting pose.

"This is going to be my greatest portrait," said van Gogh.

Without saying another word, van Gogh drew a charcoal sketch of his model and positioned it on the canvas. As he glanced at the sketch and back at his model, he realized that her folded arms and body language were telling him she was upset.

It was Agostina who broke the stillness. "Vincent, we must talk."

"Okay, but stay tranquil, and do not move a muscle," said van Gogh, painting furiously.

"Vincent, I don't think I can go on with this. My nerves are destroyed." Her eyes, once sparkling, looked tired.

"If you are referring to that Mignotte, he had better not show up here again."

"No, Vincent, we have to break this off." She shifted in her seat as she took a sip from her mug.

"Why, Agostina? No, please, I need you in my life," Vincent pleaded as he set down his brush.

"Van Gogh, I am pregnant."

Without thinking, Vincent answered, "Is that so disheartening? It should be exhilarating news."

"Oh, God! Do you live in another world? It could be Mignotte's kid or yours." Agostina broke her pose altogether and leaned forward.

"In any case, you're still expecting a child," answered van Gogh.

"You don't understand!" she blurted out. "Mignotte has already demanded that I get an abortion and leave Paris. After all, the son of a bitch is in charge of the dieu damne Morals Brigade!"

"Agostina, we can raise the child together."

"No, he's threatened to put me in prison and deport you. Besides, I'm afraid you will do something drastic. You're an emotional man who can easily get out of control. Vincent, it's over. It's not your concern anymore," yelled Agostina standing from the chair and running to the back of the café.

The artist no longer felt like finishing the painting. He put the canvas under his arm, left the café, and returned to his flat on Rue Lepic. Theo was not at home, so he walked to Tanguy's shop at Rue Clauzel. From outside, van Gogh could see several art students looking at brushes and other supplies inside the shop.

When van Gogh opened the door, Julien Tanguy turned to greet him. "Ah, mon ami, what can I do for you today?"

"Julien, I must speak with you about a matter of confidence."

"Oui, Vincent, come in the back where we won't be disturbed."

As the men walked to the back of the shop, van Gogh whispered, "Julien, I need a pistol. An insane person in my neighborhood wants to kill me. I need something for protection."

"Vincent, are you sure you need a gun?"

"Oui, père, I am sure."

"Well then, there's a man on Rue Lepic right near your flat," said Tanguy. "Augi Latouche sells anything you may need. He lives over the *boulangerie* at number twenty-three Lepic."

"Thank you, Père Tanguy. I'm in a desperate situation."

"Okay, but be careful my boy, and only use the gun in self-defense."

As Vincent left the shop and headed toward Rue Lepic, he heard someone yelling to him from across the street.

"Gogh! Where are you going? It's me, Lautrec."

"Oh, Henri, I just stopped at Tanguy's to see how my paintings are selling."

"That bad? Say, you don't look that well, Vincent. You could use a drink, and it's already the green hour."

The two men sat in a bistro on Rue Clauzel and ordered absinthe, raide, with a few cubes of sugar and two glasses of brandy. As the men drank, Henri became very talkative, while Vincent just listened. The Dutchman did not want to tell Henri what he was contemplating.

"Vincent, I'm glad we got together this evening. I've got to tell you about Suzanne."

"Why, what's happened?"

"She tried to commit suicide last night."

"What?"

"Oui, she tried to take poison, but we took her to a doctor, who pumped her stomach and saved her."

"How did all this start? What was the cause?"

"Well, as you know, we have been living together off and on in her mother's house. One day, I came home and heard her mother balling her out for ruining their plan to get me to marry Suzanne."

"They had a plan?"

"Yes, do you believe it? I heard the old lady yelling at her for going out with Louis Anquetin and messing up the plan."

"Henri, are you sure it was Louis?"

"Well, to tell you the truth, I asked Louis to take her off my hands. She was getting too close. He only screwed her as a personal favor to me."

"You're really a strange man, Henri."

"Let me get back to the story. I burst in on their discussion and told both of them that I would never marry Suzanne and that I'm disappointed over her affair with Louis. The next thing I know, she's rolling around the floor and foaming at the mouth. Her mother and I took her down the street to Dr. Cabanne."

"Are you going to see her again?"

"Are you crazy? I don't want to go near those people ever again. Besides, I don't ever want to get married."

Henri's story about Suzanne got Vincent to share his own news. "Henri, Agostina's pregnant, and Mignotte told her to get an abortion and get out of Paris. He also wants to deport me to the Netherlands."

"Wow, my problems are nothing compared to yours. What are you going to do?"

"I'm going to kill that fuck, Mignotte. It's the only way Agostina can ever be free of him."

"Vincent, that won't help anything. You'll be a criminal. They'll catch you, and you'll get the guillotine."

"I then plan to kill myself. Life holds nothing for me."

"Vincent, how can you say that? Just look at your art. It's blossoming. Your paintings are brimming with color. You have finally learned how to express your soul and the world around you."

"It's no use. I've made up my mind."

"No, Vincent, I know this Mignotte. I know what makes him tick. It's all a show. He's this moral, religious conservative on the outside, but beneath it all he's the lowest of the low. Why do you think he was at Le Tambourin in the morning? He makes a bunch of stops during the day, and then at night he's home with the religious wife and family. He keeps his job by kissing the ass of his monsignor, Père Tralbout, and the mayor of Montmartre."

To calm Henri's concern, van Gogh said, "You may be right about this Mignotte; he's not worth killing. Henri, I have to get back to Rue Lepic. I have an appointment. I'll see you tomorrow."

32

"Oh yeah, you're the Dutch artist who lives with his brother at number fifty-four. What do you want the gun for?" asked Augi Latouche as he unwrapped the burlap cloth from the steel gray pistol. It was dark in the alley behind the boulangerie, but a gaslight on Rue Lepic shed some light on the transaction.

"I have to settle a score with one of Montmartre's leading citizens," said van Gogh as he felt the weight of the gun in his hand.

"That will be six francs for the pistol and the bullets."

Van Gogh made the exchange, walked out of the alley onto Rue Lepic, and disappeared into the night. He was not aware that he had just purchased a weapon from a police informant in the employ of the Morals Brigade.

Vincent walked down the hill to Place Blanche, the base of La Buttes. The pistol felt hard and cold as it rested between his waist and his belt. The artist walked directly down the boulevard to the police precinct on Rue Blanche, off Boulevard de Clichy. From across the street, he could see that Mignotte's office was dark. A gendarme manned the front desk, but Vincent could not see any supervising officers in the building; they apparently only worked during the daytime.

Van Gogh's plan was to wait for Mignotte in his darkened office until morning. When the prefect arrived, Vincent would shoot him and then turn the gun on himself. No one would be held responsible, and Mignotte and Vincent van Gogh would cease to exist.

As he approached the front desk of the precinct, the gendarme stopped him. "May I help you, monsieur? What is the problem?"

Van Gogh's mind went blank. He had a story about picking up a package from the prefect's office, but he could not find the words to make the deception believable. Instead, he asked to use the water closet, but the officer told him to use the street—the restroom was kept closed during the night.

Vincent walked down the sidewalk away from the police station. He circled the block. Looking again at the entrance to the station, he thought, "Maybe, I'll wait until morning and shoot Mignotte when he arrives for work tomorrow. But wait—if I kill him, the police will say that Agostina was involved in the crime, and she'll be punished."

Van Gogh was not sure what he should do. However, he was tired, both physically and mentally, so he decided to go home and get some rest.

When he arrived at number fifty-four Rue Lepic, he noticed that the large, wooden doors leading to the courtyard of his building were open. He could see two uniformed gendarmes and Prefect Mignotte getting out of a horse-drawn police van, parked by the entrance. Most men would have left the scene, but not this Dutchman.

At a distance, Vincent followed the policemen into the building and up the stairs. Finally, van Gogh heard the police prefect's voice coming from above. "We are here to speak with Vincent van Gogh, the artist. Is he at home this evening?"

As Vincent slowly ascended the stairs, he saw Mignotte and the two uniformed gendarmes standing outside the door to his flat with their pistols drawn. The door slowly opened, and Theo announced in a nervous tone, "I am Theodore van Gogh, his brother. Has he done anything wrong?"

"That's for us to know. Just answer the question. Is he at home?"

"No, he is not, and I don't know where he is."

The police officers continued their interrogation from the hallway and asked Theo where the artist went in the evening. Suddenly, Vincent appeared at the doorway behind the policemen. The men turned and grabbed him, pinning him to the wall with their pistols. All three searched him for a weapon, ripping his pockets in the process.

"You bought a pistol. Did you think you would kill me?" asked Mignotte.

Vincent was momentarily stunned by the revelation that his purchase of the gun had not been as secret as he had supposed. He had to think quickly. "I was going to kill myself," he said, which was partly true, "but I threw it in the river. You see, I do not have it anymore."

Just then, Henri hobbled out into the hallway. "Gentlemen, I am Count Henri de Toulouse Lautrec Manfa. Will you please come back into the flat and close the door."

With their guns still drawn, the police marched Vincent into the apartment and closed the door.

Once everyone was inside, Henri continued. "Prefect Mignotte, Monsieur van Gogh will not harm you. But the damage to your reputation has been profound."

"What do you refer to, Monsieur Lautrec?"

"Mademoiselle Agostina Segatori carries your child."

The two gendarmes looked at each other and put their pistols back in their holsters.

Henri continued. "And I have spoken to the young lady. The story will never go any further than the walls of this flat. I see no need to inform my cousin George Clemenceau, the former mayor of Montmartre, or your parish monsignor, Père Tralbout, of your indiscretion. All I ask is that you forget about this situation and leave these people alone. I assure you, prefect, there will be no further trouble."

Mignotte was speechless, and his face turned ashen gray, for he knew that Henri had many powerful connections. A scandal would certainly cost him his job. "Okay, it's agreed. But I must inform you that the Café du Tambourin has been padlocked this evening for bankruptcy, failure to pay creditors. The bitch is out of business. No one can get in there anymore."

With that, Mignotte and the gendarmes turned on their heels and left the flat. Theo ran to his brother and hugged him.

Emile, who was also in the flat, went to van Gogh and grabbed him around his lapels. "Vincent, what were you trying to do? I heard from Tanguy that you bought a pistol and I immediately came to your flat. Where is the gun?"

"When I saw the police coach downstairs, I hid the gun in the courtyard by the turnaround. But don't worry. I don't think I could actually shoot another human being. Besides, I came to realize that Agostina could have been implicated and put into prison."

"Well, they have closed down her café. How will she get along?" asked Henri.

"I heard she has saved her money wisely over the years," said Theo. "Perhaps, she'll go back to Italy with her mother."

Henri looked at Vincent and hit him lightly with his cane. "You thick Dutchman. Why did you almost throw it all away with your uncontrollable anger? We all agree that you have finally hit your stride. Your paintings are full of life and dazzling competence."

Vincent smiled at the compliment but sadly replied, "I loved the woman, and now I've lost her forever."

33

For the first night since it had opened, Café du Tambourin was completely silent and dark. In the middle of the night, Vincent walked down to the café and found a large chain and padlock securing the front door. A paper warning sign was plastered across the door, declaring the premises in default of bankruptcy and forbidding anyone from entering. Looking through the window, Vincent could vaguely see his paintings in a pile in the middle of the empty floor.

He ran the few blocks to Agostina's flat on Rue de Douai. All the lights were out, but Vincent still knocked loudly on the door. He woke up the landlord, who let him in, and the artist banged on Agostina's door on the second floor until she opened it.

Agostina was in her nightgown and carried a small lamp. Its light illuminated her deathly pale face and tired body.

"Van Gogh, what are you doing here? I told you to leave me alone."

"You look terrible, Tina, what happened?"

"I no longer have the child."

"Oh no, that's a terrible thing."

"I had a miscarriage. I don't want to discuss it any further. Just leave me alone, and get out of my life."

"But Mignotte has agreed to leave us alone. He made a deal with Henri."

"I don't care if you made deal with the devil. I don't want to see you anymore."

A teenage boy in pajamas appeared in the living room. Rubbing his eyes, he attempted to recognize the visitor speaking with his mother.

"Mama, who is this man?"

Looking at Vincent, Agostina said, "Vincent, this is my son, Jean-Pierre."

"You have a son? You never told me. Where was he all this time?"

"He lives with my aunt and her family here in Paris."

Looking stunned and confused, Vincent asked, "Why did you never tell me? Did I mean that little to you?"

"A café is no place to raise a son. When my mother got too old to take care of Jean-Pierre, my Aunt Marie brought him to live with her family in the Montparnasse district."

"You know what kind of man I am. Having a child would not have made any difference to me."

"I just felt that our affair would never go any place, and Jean-Pierre was my own business."

Vincent looked over at the boy and did not know what to say. He finally responded, "I guess I really never got to know you, did I, Tina?"

"No, you didn't. Now get out, and don't come back."

"But … but can I get my canvases back from the café?"

"I don't know about your paintings. The city officials told me no one was allowed to take anything from Le Tambourin under the terms of the bankruptcy. I guess your canvases go the way of the café for legal reasons."

Vincent knew that the affair with Agostina was indeed over. But now, he felt more upset over the paintings that he had left in the café. It was safer to place his art above the people in his life, thus avoiding despair and disappointment. Vincent never did get the paintings back. They were sold later at a bankruptcy auction for a few centimes each.

Van Gogh was glad, however, that he had taken the unfinished portrait of Agostina out of the café the last time he had been there. He would paint the rest from memory, remembering all the marvelous colors in her clothing and within the café.

34

After the traumatic breakup with Agostina, van Gogh's relationship with Theo also appeared to disintegrate. He started drinking heavily and became more introverted, and he took out his unhappiness on his brother.

When he did come home, Vincent would wake Theo with senseless talk about the art market. The monologue would last late into the night. During this time, he also berated his brother for not selling any of his paintings.

Theo could not cope with Vincent's behavior. He tried to avoid his erratic sibling by spending time with Andries Bonger, a friend from Amsterdam who was living in Paris. On several occasions, he and Andries traveled to Amsterdam. On one such trip, Theo met Andries' younger sister, Johanna. He instantly felt a loving bond toward the young woman, who was studying to become an English teacher. She was petite with youthful features and brown eyes and hair.

Vincent became enraged when Theo spoke affectionately about Johanna. He was threatened by her existence. What was once a straight line had become a triangle. Vincent did not know how he could share his brother's attention with another human being.

Emile Bernard decided to spend the summer in Brittany and Pont-Aven painting with Paul Gauguin. They asked van Gogh to join them, but the Dutchman said he wanted to stay in Paris and paint in the vicinity of Asniers.

Henri Toulouse-Lautrec also went off on his own. He began experimenting with lithography, or printing posters from metal plates for business clients who wanted publicity. One of his first customers was Aristide Bruant, the comedian/singer. Henri created some cover illustrations for his sheet music and, later, posters advertising his appearances at various café-concerts around Montmartre.

Despite his inner turmoil or perhaps because of his mental state, van Gogh became even more compulsively involved with his painting. Without restraint, he entertained all manner of novel impulses and absurd ideas. His paintings became a simultaneous translation of his own anxiety, rage, joy, and depression. Forceful color and bold composition became his means of expression.

During one of his lone forays into the northern suburbs, the artist happened to see Paul Signac, the pointillist painter and friend of George Seurat. Paul was involved in a painting along the Seine, near Asniers, and looked up when van

Gogh came into view. Theo had introduced Signac to Vincent during the previous summer.

"Aren't you Vincent, the brother of Theo van Gogh of Boussod & Valadon?"

"Oui, it's my only claim to fame. My painting, apparently, is still a secret," said van Gogh in a depressed tone.

"Oh, no, I've heard about your painting. People say you have your own expressive style that is like no other."

"Merci, monsieur, that is very kind of you." Van Gogh watched Signac as he precisely applied the numerous dots of color to his painting. "You know, Paul, I have incorporated this technique into some of my painting, but on its own, it's too structured and scientific for me. It eliminates both the expressionism and the emotionalism in my art."

"All painters must discover their own artistic idiom," said Signac. "When you stand back from your painting, it is only you who must be satisfied."

"Oui," responded the Dutchman, "painting is a faith, and it imposes the duty to disregard public opinion."

Van Gogh liked Signac, and the two painted many times during the spring and summer around Asnieres. During this period, Vincent painted a number of river scenes, restaurants, and still lifes in the pointillist style, but his technique was never as precise or scientific as that of Paul Signac.

During his last summer in Montmartre, Vincent took all of the influences—academic, Impressionism, Japonisme, pointillism, and the theories of his fellow Parisian artists—and put them together in his own style, which he termed "Vincentism." This integration, plus his work with flower still lifes and the influence of Monticelli and Gauguin, had found a way into the Dutchman's unique technique and outlook.

With glowing candles on his straw hat, he would often paint far into the night. Van Gogh realized it was risky, but the danger kept him awake. Furthermore, in this strange light, he was always in the company of the green fairy. Vincent had become convinced that the hallucinations and paranoia that he suffered while drinking increased his sensual awareness and expressionism in his paintings.

When Emile Bernard returned to Paris after the summer, he found a very tired Vincent van Gogh, exhausted from all the frenzied hours of painting and the increased use of alcohol. But Vincent was also tiring of Montmartre and Paris. He complained about the beginning of the cooler weather, the effects of bad food on his stomach, and the infighting among artists trying to sell their paintings.

The Dutchman had convinced himself that Marseille and Provence were actually Japon, full of colorful light and sensual women. He had created a fantasy that he was convinced would become real if he could travel to the south. It was in this land of enchantment where he thought he could paint his first marvelous masterpiece.

35

A chilly February breeze was blowing as Emile helped Vincent carry his suitcases toward the Gare de Lyon railway station to catch a train to Marseille. It was a cold, gray day, similar to the one van Gogh had found on his arrival in Paris almost twenty-four months earlier. He never discussed his leaving with Theo. Instead, he left his paintings scattered around the apartment as if he were coming back. Van Gogh knew he would not be able to leave Theo if he had to face him.

"Why can't you stay?" asked Emile. "The winter will pass, and we'll have the wonderful spring to paint in the country."

"No, my time in Paris is over. Theo should be alone. He'll probably get married. I would become a burden and get in the way." When they arrived at the train track, van Gogh embraced his friend. "You take care of yourself, Emile. I'm off to encounter fame and fortune."

As Vincent placed his belongings above his seat in the compartment, he could see Emile Bernard waiting on the platform for the train to leave. As Emile waved *au revoir*, the train pulled away, and a tear came to van Gogh's eye. Somehow, he knew that he and his best friend would never meet again.

When the train pulled out of the station, van Gogh remembered his journey to Paris two years before. He had made a pact with himself to learn how to express the art inside him. Despite his inner turmoil, he felt that he had accomplished his goal and could now create a successful *oeuvre* of his paintings.

Vincent had intended to go to Marseille, but when he saw Arles through the window, he decided to detrain. Arles was an old, Roman city in Provence surrounded by sunflowers, vineyards, corn, and lavender fields. He had arrived at his utopia, his *Japon*.

Van Gogh stayed in Arles and Provence for about two years before traveling north and living near Paris. However, it would prove to be the most painful yet productive time in his life.

Epilogue

It was a dry, sunny day when Emile Bernard arrived in the village of Auvers, about eighteen miles north of Paris. While stepping from the train, he noticed that the towering church with its semicircular apse dominated the sky. Notre Dame d'Auvers dated back to the twelfth century and was huge in comparison to the size of the town. The air was still and quiet, as if the village was mourning for one of its own.

The town and its church were built on a hill overlooking the river Oise, an ideal location for the river scenes favored by many artists over the years. Corot, Daubigny, Monet, and Renoir were just a few of the artists who had come here to paint. Tilting his head upward, Emile could see a stately chateau above the town with wheat fields beyond. From the railroad station, it was short walk to the small café and inn of Arthur Ravoux in the center of town.

The inn was a square, two-story structure painted maroon and white. No one sat at the tables and chairs outside its entrance. But the door to the inn was open, and the front shutters were tightly closed.

Upon entering the establishment, Emile was engaged by the strong aroma of freshly cut flowers. The large room that made up the café was filled with mourners. Local folk in modest clothing mingled with city dwellers in black frock jackets and formal trousers.

Emile quickly recognized Julien Tanguy and Theo and walked over to them. He offered Theo his condolences, and the men embraced. It had been over two years since Emile had seen Theo and he looked very much older and quite thin. His red eyes accentuated his pallid complexion. Other mourners arrived, and Theo excused himself to go over to greet them.

As Emile turned, he was gripped by the sight of Vincent's casket covered by a simple, white cloth. The bier, located across the room, was surrounded with masses of flowers: sunflowers, yellow dahlias, and yellow irises. Yellow flowers were everywhere. After all, yellow was his favorite color.

Above the closed casket, some of Vincent's paintings hung on the wall, making a sort of halo for him. They included *The Irises, The Church of Auvers, Wheatfield with Crows, The Child with an Orange,* and a strange painting of convicts walking in a circle surrounded by high prison walls. One of the unhappy convicts looked like Vincent himself.

His easel, his folding stool, and his brushes had been lovingly placed in front of the coffin. Upon seeing them, Emile thought about all the times the two had painted together in Montmartre, and he began to cry.

"Emile, what a shame," said Tanguy. "The brilliance and genius of these paintings makes his death even more painful."

"Why now, Julien? I heard he was doing well up here in Auvers."

"I guess it was all too much for the passionate Dutchman. I understand he had many epileptic seizures and mental breakdowns during the two years he was on his own in Arles."

"But his painting has become brilliant," replied Emile. "These are all masterpieces of color and light."

"Emile," said Tanguy in a low voice, "I heard he shot himself near the heart, in the fields behind the chateau. He used the same pistol he purchased in Montmartre during that incident with the police prefect."

Emile and Tanguy were interrupted by a dignified and melancholy man in his sixties. "Monsieur Bernard, I am Dr. Paul Gachet. I was Vincent's physician. He often spoke of you as a true friend."

Tears welled up in Emile's eyes as he imagined Vincent confiding his feelings to the doctor. Through his tears, Emile asked, "What would make him do this terrible thing, Dr. Gachet?"

"That is difficult to say. Vincent was a very tormented individual. After a year at the asylum in Saint-Remy de Provence, he came here to Auvers and was placed under my supervision."

"To be close to Paris and his brother?"

"Yes. A few times he rode the train into the city to see Theo, but he always rushed back to Auvers."

"Did he rush back because the pressure and stress of Paris was too much?"

"No," answered Gachet, "he became very upset over the well-being of Theo and his family—his wife, Johanna, and their baby son, Vincent Willem."

"Yes, I was in Brittany when I received a letter from Vincent telling me how proud he was to have the baby named after him. He never told me about the problems Theo was having."

More people began arriving, including Paul Laval, Lucien Pissarro, and almost two dozen other artists and friends from van Gogh's Paris days. Henri Toulouse-Lautrec was traveling abroad and did not know of his friend's passing. The local people in the room had only known Vincent for about two months, having seen him sitting at his easel in the fields and around the town.

One of the local residents introduced himself to Emile. "Hello, I'm Jacques Levert, a carpenter here in Auvers. Vincent was a gentle man, who always had a kind word even for a stranger. I'd see him often, painting frantically in the hills around town. I hear that you were his best friend, monsieur. Why was he in such a hurry?"

"I think he painted in a hurry because he wanted to express the art inside him before it could be corrected or changed by his intellect."

"You mean, he was a free spirit?"

"Oui, Jacques, that is a perfect description of the man."

Emile noticed that Theo was alone, and he excused himself from the carpenter. "Theo, my friend, how are you holding up?"

"Oh, Emile, I still can't believe this has happened. I was with him all night before he died."

"Couldn't anything be done to save him?"

"No, the doctors said he had lost too much blood. Besides, Vincent said he wanted to die and would only try again."

"He must have been so weary of life," said Emile, "after all he had been through."

"Yes, my friend, but in his troubled mind, he thought this tragedy would benefit me." Theo started to cry loudly but he fought back the tears and continued his conversation with Emile. "He loved little Vincent, his nephew, and he found out I was not feeling well and having financial difficulties at the gallery. My brother fully believed that his monthly allowance could be better used for the family's survival."

At three o'clock, the body was moved by a horse-drawn hearse to a small, new cemetery outside of Auvers. In the hot sun, the mourners followed the casket as it was carried up a little hill overlooking the fields, which were ripe for harvest. There was a wide, blue sky above, and Emile remembered how much Vincent loved the hot sun in his face. He recalled that he had once referred to sunshine as "a gift from God."

Author's Note

Theo van Gogh was heartbroken and never got over the death of his brother, who was only thirty-seven. Theo died himself six months later of complications from a liver infection and a stroke. He was laid to rest in Utrecht in the Netherlands. However, in 1914, Johanna had her husband's body reburied next to Vincent van Gogh's grave in the cemetery near Auvers. She came to realize that Theo was the central force in the artist's life and should share in his accomplishments. There was no better place for him to rest in peace.

During his stay in Auvers, van Gogh painted more than seventy-five works in two months. His physician, Dr. Paul Gachet, sat for two portraits during this time. One of these paintings was auctioned at Christie's for more than US $82.5 million in 1990.

978-0-595-44160-
0-595-44160-2

Lightning Source UK Ltd.
Milton Keynes UK
UKHW011139090621
385205UK00001B/70